MISCHIEF

Mischief

"Candy is dandy," Nora said with a sigh of pleasure. "But to lick her is quicker."

When Mistress Nora's young French lover Nico admits he's always wanted to celebrate a real American Halloween, she summons him to Halloween Town, USA—a.k.a. Salem, Massachusetts—for two nights of sex and candy.

If necessary, they can skip the candy.

This Original Sinners Pulp Library edition of *Mischief* also includes "Coming and Going," a bonus short story featuring Mistress Nora and Nico.

MISCHIEF

TIFFANY REISZ

8TH CIRCLE PRESS • LOUISVILLE, KY

Dedicated to Andrew Shaffer

Happy Halloweener!

CONTENTS

MISCHIEF

A HALLOWEEN NOVELLA

I t all started with an innocent question. In a letter to Nico, Mistress Nora wrote, *Americans envy the French their fashion sense, cheese, wine, and romantic language. What do the French envy about America and Americans?*

Nico's answer surprised her.

I can't speak for the whole country, but for me, I envy your Halloween. We don't have a holiday like it in France. I've always wanted to experience a real American Halloween.

Of course, Nora knew they didn't have Halloween in France any more than America had Bastille Day. But it had never occurred to her that Nico or any other Frenchman would envy a children's holiday that meant nothing more than an evening of costumes, candy, and legally-sanctioned bad behavior.

She'd written Nico back—snail mail, as it was her lover's preferred method of communication—and asked him what specifically it was about Halloween he envied. A reply arrived two weeks later.

Candy, he'd said.

Costumes, of course.

Legally-sanctioned bad behavior.

She should have guessed.

In France, as a kid in school, Nico wrote, *we studied Halloween. We had to practice saying "trick or treat" in English. In French it translates to something more like "candy or mischief." American movies make it look fun and crazy, but every October thirty-first came and went without any mischief or candy.*

Her poor boy. Nora decided she would most certainly be the absolute worst domme in the known world if she didn't give her darling French submissive his first real American Halloween. He was twenty-six, about a decade her junior. But it was long overdue. She knew she was spoiling her boy, but what was the fun of owning your own personal gorgeous French vintner if you didn't get to spoil him a little every now and then?

Thus Operation Candy and Mischief commenced.

Step one involved persuading Nico to fly

to America. She hadn't expected this would be too difficult, as his winery's harvest had ended in mid-September. Even if he was still preoccupied with work at the end of October, she could order him to come visit her in the States—one of the perks of the dominatrix trade. Of course, it didn't come to that. He was game for anything, as long as he got to see her again.

Step two involved finding somewhere in the US where they could stay for a few days and go Halloween-crazy. It had to be somewhere that celebrated Halloween for several days, not just the thirty-first. There were two options: West Hollywood, or Salem, Massachusetts. Nico wanted the full American Halloween experience and that meant crisp autumn weather, leaves changing colors on the trees, smoking chimneys, and apple cider. So Salem it was.

Just out of curiosity, Nora asked Nico what else he envied about American culture.

His answer? Cheerleaders.

Apparently, French sports didn't have cheerleaders, and Nico found the whole concept rather sexy and exotic. Well, now Nora knew what she'd be wearing on All Hallow's Eve.

Step three meant cramming together

twenty-six years of Halloween experiences into the three days Nico could spare away from the winery. They were too old for door-to-door trick-or-treating, but Nora had a few other plans in mind. After all, no one was ever too old for candy and mischief.

Especially not her.

Not so coincidentally, the dates of their vacation coincided with a conference her own master, Søren, had to attend in Petaluma, California. The topic was something incredibly boring like "Jesuits Helping Build a Bridge of Compassion Into the Future."

"Bridges of compassion?" Søren had said with disgust. "I remember when Jesuits were still the terrifying priests in the Church."

"Don't worry, sir," Nora said. "You still scare the holy living shit out of everyone you meet."

"Thank you," he said. "Coming from you that is high praise indeed."

She told him she'd be out of town as well while he was gone. He knew better than to ask why. Nora was a "switch," one of those rare BDSM unicorns who was both a submissive and a dominant. When she felt the urge to swing a crop instead of take one, she had Nico. Søren was no switch, but he had his own private Frenchman—Kingsley, who just happened to be Nico's father.

True story.

Nora and Søren had made a pact to give each other privacy with their respective pets, lest things become awkward. Or more awkward, at least. The system worked well enough, except for the occasional hiccup.

One hiccup occurred when Søren walked into her bedroom on October third and caught her trying on a cheerleading uniform. He stared at her as if he'd never seen a thirty-seven-year-old woman wearing a New Orleans Saints cheerleader uniform, her black hair in an obnoxiously high ponytail, wearing white tennis shoes and bobby socks, standing in the middle of what was supposed to be a dominatrix's wicked red bedroom. He paused, seemed to want to say something, then clearly thought better of it.

"Don't ask," she said to him. "Just...for your own good, don't ask."

Without another word, he left her all alone in the room. For about three seconds.

Then he came back in, pointed at the outfit and said, "Keep that one for later," before leaving again.

Men.

During a planning phone call, Nora couldn't get Nico to tell her what his Halloween costume was because he wanted to surprise her. She told him not to dress up like his father in a Regency suit, since that's how Søren had dressed last Halloween. And she told him not to dress as a priest, since that's how Kingsley had dressed.

"They traded clothes for Halloween?" Nico asked.

"Um...yes," she said.

"One day you're going to explain their relationship to me," Nico said.

Nora considered this request. "Do I have to?"

Nico promised he'd dress as neither a priest nor a king. She could have ordered him to tell her his costume, but where was the fun in that? If he wanted to be mischievous, well, mischief was the entire point of the trip, wasn't it?

And candy.

Of course candy. Mischief and candy were the two entire points of the trip and nothing else.

Except for sex. Lots and lots of sex. That was also the point of the trip.

Mischief and candy and sex.

If necessary, they could skip the candy.

The second Nora arrived in Salem, a few hours ahead of Nico, the old familiar, homey atmosphere of New England fall enveloped her. She was wearing her favorite gray wool slacks, a cozy black turtleneck, and her cat-eye frame glasses. Her hair was up in a loose bun. Her seat mate on the flight had guessed she was a librarian. Nora said, "Close enough."

She'd once fucked a librarian. (Okay, more than once.) Surely that counted for something.

After stopping for supplies—wine and candy and lube—she drove to the Victorian B&B where she'd rented the honeymoon suite for her and Nico. Mr. Sheldon, the owner of the B&B, met her at her car with a welcoming smile. He was late middle-age, balding, bespectacled and be-sweatered. Nora tried to stop him from lifting her luggage, but he waved her off, which he came to regret immediately.

"Oh my," he said, his face reddening as he hefted her black leather toy bag. "What on earth do you have in here? Bowling balls?"

"Floggers, canes, whips, handcuffs. But the

real heavy things in there are the spreader bars. They're made of steel."

The man stared at her blankly. He blinked slowly.

"I'm a dominatrix," she said, taking the toy bag back from him. "For Halloween."

"Ah!" her host said, his face lighting up with delight. "Wonderful idea. I usually go as a rock star. I have a big Bon Jovi wig. Horrifies the grandkids, which is half the fun of it. What do you do in real life?"

"I'm…" She pondered that question for a split second. "…a librarian."

"I could have guessed. You're an angel all year and you get to be wicked for one night. Or two," he said with a little wink.

"Right," Nora said as he showed her up to the suite. "Or two."

He gave her the keys and wished her a pleasant stay.

"My boyfriend's going to arrive around eight, I think," Nora said before he left, "unless his flight is late. So if a really handsome guy who looks too young for me shows up on your doorstep, that's him. You can send him up."

"Where's he coming in from?"

"France," she said. "He's never celebrated

Halloween before. I'm trying to give him the grand tour."

"What's on the agenda?"

"He had three requests since we're both a little old for trick-or-treating. He wants to go to a costume party."

"Easy enough. You can't go five feet downtown without running into someone in costume."

"And he wants to visit a haunted house, the cheesier the better," Nora said.

"We have them by the dozens."

"The third one might be a little difficult. I'm ninety percent sure he was kidding, but… he says he wants to see a ghost."

Her host didn't seem particularly surprised by that. Living in Salem, he probably heard stranger things from tourists.

"Hmm…" he said, nodding and stroking the non-existent beard on his non-existent chin. "A ghost. Well, there's always St. Patrick's. If there's a ghost in town, that's where you'll find her."

"St. Patrick's? A church? Hospital?"

"Cemetery," he said. "Catholic."

"Does St. Patrick's have a ghost?"

"The Smiling Girl," he said. "Went to meet her boyfriend there for you-know-what. Got stabbed by a madman instead. Supposedly when they found her body she was smiling. People say she'll walk up next to you if you're foolish enough to take a stroll through the graveyard at midnight."

"Perfect," Nora said. "I am definitely foolish enough."

CHAPTER TWO

While Nora waited for Nico's arrival, she unpacked and got settled into their temporary home. Their suite took up the entire third floor of The Painted Lady B&B. The floors were honey-colored hardwood, covered in faded rugs. The living room was cozy, with an antique sofa. The floor-to-ceiling bookshelves were filled with travel guides, novels set in Salem and Boston, and non-fiction books about the town's dark history with witches. The bedroom had a gas-log fireplace and a queen-sized Colonial canopy bed covered in an antique Amish bedspread.

Nora tested the four posts of the bed. It was sturdy as iron. She hopped up and down on the mattress and heard nary a squeak. A well-made piece of furniture. She and Nico would have very good—and very quiet sex—in this bed. But she needed to remember to take the bedspread off first. The Amish might not appreciate it if they got semen stains on their handcrafted quilt. Or maybe they would appreciate it? She'd never met an Amish person. They could be kinky motherfuckers, too. Who knew?

Evening came and Nora showered and changed into something more comfortable—her favorite short black silk nightgown and matching robe. When that was done there wasn't much left to do but pace the suite while waiting for Nico's cab to arrive.

She would have picked him up at the airport, but he declined the offer. He preferred to keep their reunions private. It was one of his little quirks. He was quiet and self-contained, but deeply emotional, and nothing made him more emotional than seeing her again after a long separation. He called the one time they reunited in an airport "miserable" (a word meant to be spoken with a French accent) and swore he'd never do it again. If he couldn't kiss her in public the way he wanted to kiss her, what was even the point of kissing? She couldn't argue with that, so she continued her pacing, phone in hand so she could answer long-neglected emails while she waited. Anything to distract her from peeking out the window every thirty seconds.

At eight, it already looked like midnight outside. For Nico, on French time, it would be the wee hours of the morning. He'd either be exhausted from his flight and want to go to sleep immediately…or he'd be wide awake from sleeping on the plane and jump her the second they were alone.

Nora put her money on the jumping. There were perks to having a twenty-six-year-old boyfriend.

At last, she saw the flash of headlights on her window. She pushed back the white lace curtain and saw Nico standing next to the yellow cab, paying the driver. He must have seen movement in the corner of his eye because he looked up to her window and smiled.

Nora waved. He kissed the air to her in greeting before hefting his bag over his shoulder and walking to the house. Her heart leapt a few inches skyward in her chest. Her stomach twisted itself into a knot. Her hands trembled, ever so slightly.

Grow up, Nora, she told herself.

It was a tiny bit embarrassing how infatuated she was with Nico. She hadn't known how much she'd needed a submissive of her very own until he'd come into her life and she discovered what she'd been missing all along. Sometimes it seemed impossible he should be hers. He was handsome, of course, like his father. The longer she knew him, however, the less he resembled Kingsley and the more he became unique and incomparable. He had deep olive skin, even darker than Kingsley's, and celadon eyes inherited from his Persian mother. His dark hair was often unruly, especially when he'd been sweating in the sun.

He dressed nothing like Kingsley, which she found all the more appealing. No suits. No ties. No military coats. No boots except for work boots, the sorts with steel toes since he was often found in his vineyard with a rake or a hoe or a shovel in his calloused hands. Jeans. T-shirts. Jackets in autumn, coats in winter. Mud on his boots in all seasons.

Her Nico.

Her property.

Her other heart.

Now she knew how Søren felt, with his twin love for her and Kingsley. Not a heart divided but a heart doubled.

Maybe that was why her chest felt so tight when she heard Nico's footsteps on the stairs. Loving Nico made her love Søren even more, because he gave her room to be herself, room to love with two hearts as she'd given him room to love her and Kingsley. When she got back from Salem and he from California, she would show him just how much that meant to her. But meanwhile…

Before Nico could knock, she opened the door for him. He stepped across the threshold, the slightest smile on his lips.

"Happy Halloween," Nora said.

"Trick or treat?" Nico asked.

Nora grinned. He was so good at this already.

"For you right now," she said, "all treats. No tricks." She reached for his hand, pulled him into the room, and shut the door behind them.

His arm was around her waist before his bag hit the floor. Nora put her hands on his face and kissed him. Eager and hungry as they both were for each other, it was something of a miracle that all they did in that first minute together was kiss.

It was no ordinary kiss. It was long and deep. Nora bit Nico's bottom lip, tasted his tongue in her mouth. Her hands caught in his hair. His hands stroked her bare neck and shoulders. By the time the kiss ended, she'd pushed his back against the door.

She couldn't hold off touching him one second longer. Nora unbuttoned and un-zipped his jeans, and grazed her fingertips lightly—ever so lightly—over the lowest part of his stomach, that nice little tender place right before things got interesting. Nico in-haled softly and Nora grinned.

"So…which do you want first?" she asked him. "Candy? Or mischief?"

Because he was such a smart man and a quick learner, he answered exactly the way she wanted him to.

"Both."

CHAPTER THREE

Nora took him by the hand and led him into the bedroom. She already had the gas log fireplace burning and the lights turned low. This was a short trip and Nora didn't want to waste a single second.

"Need anything before I tie you to this bed and leave you there for about an hour?" she asked him.

"Only you." He bent to kiss her again and during the kiss he untied the sash of her robe. He delicately stroked her sides and back with his fingertips, and the tickling sensation through the silk was utterly delicious.

"Did you miss me?" she said. "It's been for-ever since we saw each other."

"Six weeks," he said. "Longer than forever."

Nora had spent a part of August and September with Nico at his vineyard, playing chatelaine. By day, she wrote, read, and helped Nico with his vines. By night, she taught Nico how to serve her. She loved the days with him almost as much as the nights. That's how she knew it was real love, even if it had complicated her life a little bit more than she'd bargained for...

"We'll make it a good two nights," she said as she touched his lips. Beautiful lips, soon to be swollen from bites and kisses.

"Good already," he said, bending to kiss her again. "Perfect already."

She didn't let him kiss her this time. Instead she stepped back to tease him and he narrowed his eyes at her in playful frustration.

She sat in the large leather club chair with a seat wide enough it could have fit two of her. She threw her bare legs over the chair arm and waved her hand at him, indicating he should undress for her viewing pleasure.

Nora could tell Nico was trying not to smile and/or roll his eyes as he removed his black jacket, folded it in half, and dropped it on the ottoman. He wore a plain white V-neck t-shirt underneath, which he pulled off without fuss or fanfare.

"You'd make a terrible male stripper," she

said, even as she admired his lovely strong chest, his lovely stronger shoulders and arms.

He knelt to take off his shoes. "I can't dance either."

"My poor Moosh," she said, using her favorite pet name for him. He'd told her his grandmother always called him that as a child since he was so quiet. *Moosh* meant "mouse" in Farsi. "It's okay. I didn't fall in love with you because of your stripping or dancing skills."

"Why did you fall in love with me?" he asked. He stood up and kicked off his jeans.

Nora looked at his tight, toned twenty-six-year-old naked body.

Then she looked at it again.

"A few reasons."

She stood up and walked to him, pressed a kiss to his bicep and breathed in the warm scent of his sun-kissed skin. When he reached for her she danced out of his reach again.

"Ah, you drive me crazy," he said.

"That's my job. Lie down on the bed on your back. Think happy thoughts."

"I am," he said. She wrapped her fingers around his erection and stroked it upward.

"I can tell."

With a put-upon sigh, the sort Frenchmen

were best at, he crawled onto the bed. He lay in the center, face up. Nora dug through her toy bag until she found the wrist and ankle cuffs she'd bought specifically to use on Nico. They were the softest, most supple leather she could find, ten times the price of any cuffs she ever used on her clients.

But Nico was hers, and he was special and it gave her enormous pleasure spoiling him even if he didn't realize she was doing it. Though his vineyard was doing well and he made enough money, he invested it all back into the company and rarely bought anything extravagant for himself. He and Kingsley were nothing alike in that regard. Kingsley had spent years being driven around in a Rolls Royce. Meanwhile, Nico drove a twenty-year-old Land Rover and had seen a Rolls Royce once. In a movie.

Before Nora wrapped the cuffs around Nico's ankles, she massaged his calves and feet for a few minutes. The feet were a personal part of the body, vulnerable. Very few people ever had their feet touched by anyone but a masseuse or pedicurist. She liked touching Nico's feet to remind him that she owned all of his body, even the most vulnerable parts. Especially the most vulnerable parts.

Nico's breath hitched as Nora rubbed his arches with her knuckles. It always took him a few minutes to get acclimated to being treated like a possession whenever they reunited. Unlike her, he had no other lovers when they were apart, nor did he want any, he'd said. He liked his quiet life. He liked his privacy. He liked giving all of himself to his vines and his wine. It took some getting used to, he confessed, to be touched again by someone other than himself. But those moments of rediscovery, of being touched again for the first time after weeks alone, he'd said, were like the first bite of an apple in autumn after a long season of waiting for them to ripen. The first might be so tart it would set your teeth on edge and make your cheeks ache. Yet nothing in the world could stop him from taking that second bite.

That he said things like that to her without shame or embarrassment was one of the reasons she'd fallen in love with him.

Nora buckled the cuff around his right ankle. Nico closed his eyes while she buckled the cuff around his left.

"You enjoy this?" she asked.

He nodded. "Who wouldn't?"

"Fools," she said. "Fools and madmen. And dominants, which are the same thing."

"You're a dominant," he reminded her.

"Yes, which is how I know."

Nico laughed softly at her, one of her favorite sounds in the world and the perfect accompaniment to cuffing his ankles to a spreader bar. She threaded rope through the ends of the bar and tied it to the bedposts, leaving Nico's legs locked open about two feet apart at the ankles. There wasn't much more in the world Nora liked looking at more than Nico tied to a bed. However, the main reason she cuffed him was because it was difficult for him to just lay there and let her service him sexually when all his instincts told him he should be the one servicing her.

They were good instincts. Usually she encouraged them. But when she wanted to play with him like a pussy with a *moosh*.

Nora slid onto the bed and straddled Nico at his waist. Immediately his arms were around her, pulling her down to him.

"This is why I have to cuff you," she said as he ran his fingers through her hair, caressed her face and neck. "You're handsy."

"How could I not be? You're beautiful. But if you want me to stop..." He dropped his hands over his head on the pillow.

"Why are you such a good submissive?"

she asked, smiling down at her beautiful boy. "Hmm? Any ideas?"

"When Rembrandt says he wants to paint your portrait, you sit down and you hold still and you say thank you to the master for picking you out of the crowd," Nico said. "That's why."

Nora wagged her finger at him. "You… you are a silver-tongued devil."

He shook his head no, and stuck his tongue out at her. It was pink, just like hers.

"Put that tongue back in my mouth where it belongs," she said before kissing him again. The kiss grew so heated so quickly that Nico forgot himself again and wrapped his arms around her.

Without warning, she rose up onto her knees, grabbed him by the wrists, and slammed them over his head into the bed. She used her full weight to hold him down and enough pressure to leave two thumbprint bruises on the sides of his arms. He inhaled sharply at the pain and went still. It wasn't often Nora showed off around Nico. She didn't have to. He was her lover, not a client, and he adored her whether she did whip tricks for him or not. But every now and then she liked to remind him what she did in her other day job.

"You like that?" she asked.

He replied with a single word: "Rembrandt."

"Just for that," she said, "I'm going to be very nice to you right now. Ready?"

He nodded.

Nora released his wrists to fetch the cuffs and the rope. When he was strapped to the bed and unable to lift his hands, she reached back into her bag of tricks and pulled out a treat.

"For my Moosh," she said. "A kiss."

And it was a kiss. A Hershey's Kiss. Dark chocolate—her favorite kind. She set it in the hollow of Nico's throat.

"I can't eat it like that," he said.

"You're not going to eat it. Not yet. You're going to lie there while I ride your cock into this bed. If you move so much it falls out, then you don't get to come tonight. And if you manage to hold still enough while I use your cock to make myself come, then you get to come. And then you get your treat."

"You're a sadist."

"You asked for candy and mischief," she said. "And that's exactly what you're going to get."

CHAPTER FOUR

Nora didn't tell Nico she'd learned this game from Søren. Except with him, it was a glass of red wine he'd set by her hip on the kitchen table at the Sacred Heart rectory instead of a candy Kiss on the throat. And she certainly didn't tell Nico the punishment for breaking one of Søren's wine glasses was far harsher than going a night without an orgasm. Nico liked Søren and respected him, but his regard for Nora's master might be tested if he knew the full extent of Søren's sadism. It was the reason they instituted their "separation of church and state" rule. Nico and Søren weren't in the same room very often, but when they were, she preferred they didn't fight. Nico was very strong, and much younger than Søren...but if he ever took a swing at her priest, Nico would end up in the emergency room. For someone who claimed to be a pacifist, Søren had a right uppercut that could put a man on his back for a week—something that Kingsley had once learned the hard way. The only bruises she wanted to see on Nico were the ones her flogger left on his back and her teeth left on his hips. Broken ribs and ruptured livers? Nobody wanted that.

What Nora did want, however, was Nico inside of her. But what was the fun in rushing? She'd already taken her panties off, so she slid down his lovely long body and straddled his hips. Nico winced in pleasure as she pressed herself against his cock. She rocked her hips slightly and grew wetter and warmer with each tight undulation. His cock stiffened even more under her, and she felt it pushing upward, trying to find a way into her. She rocked back and forth, back and forth, bathing Nico in warm wetness. She watched his face, his eyelids fluttering in his arousal. He was likely already dying to come. Of his own volition—she certainly never gave the order—Nico never masturbated for the three days before she visited him or he her. He wasn't a classic masochist. He enjoyed the intimate attention of a flogging but didn't crave pain. But he did have a deep-seated propensity for self-denial. Her own priestly lover wasn't nearly as monkish as Nico could be at times. Another one of his little quirks. She wrote them all down in her mind inside a book she called *My Nico's Beautiful Secrets.* She kept a book for Søren, though his had a different title: *Søren's Dark Fantasies.*

Nico's book didn't have a lock on it.

Søren's did.

"Does it feel good?" she asked, already knowing the answer but wanting to hear him speak.

"Yes," he said. "Too good. If I come too soon what will you do to me?"

"The cruelest, most sadistic thing I can think of," she said. "I won't let you have any candy this entire trip. Not. One. Piece."

He feigned a look of horror, his eyes wide, his mouth open.

Nora didn't know whether to laugh or kiss him. She went with both. After a good hard laugh, she dipped her head and kissed him, but carefully, so as not to send their other Kiss tumbling to the bed.

"Now that's good," he said.

"What is?"

"Hearing you laugh. Seeing you smile."

"You missed me?" she asked, smiling down at him.

"Every day. Every night."

"You miss this?" She arched her back so the tip of Nico's cock would slide into her. His breath hitched in his throat again.

"Every night," he said.

"Not every day?"

"If I thought about your pussy during the day, I'd never get any work done."

"No more wine?"

"No more wine."

"Ah, for the best then. It's night here in Salem. You can think about my pussy all you want now. It's certainly thinking about you."

Nora proved her point by sliding all the way down the shaft, taking it deep inside of her. Nico's head fell back on the pillow and he bared his beautiful neck to her. The Kiss stayed in place in the hollow of his throat. Not that she was paying much attention to it anymore. Nico inside her was better than candy.

Nora sat up on his hips and moaned softly as Nico's cock shifted inside her, brushing against her cervix. It wasn't particularly physically pleasurable, but simply knowing he was deep in her, as deep as he could be, aroused her to distraction. Her eyes fluttered as she moved her hips in a slow oval, letting the base of his cock graze her clitoris again and again.

Strapped down to the bed as he was, Nico couldn't do much, especially not with the balancing act she'd forced on him. But nothing could stop him from tilting his hips as she rode him, fucking her from underneath. He was a sight for sore eyes, that beautiful warm brown skin of his, his taut stomach and his lovely ribcage, his toned arms over his head and tied to the bed, his lips slightly parted and his chest rising and falling with his every little hungry breath...and every inch of him hers, all hers.

Although since he was French, she supposed it ought to be every centimeter of him...

"I'm torn," she said.

"I'm not that big," Nico said.

Nora looked down at him through narrowed eyes and shook her head. "I'm torn between riding your cock so hard I come in the next two minutes," she said, "or going very slow on you so you don't lose this little game."

"If you come," he said, "I win even if I lose."

"Then you say something like that and I want to play nice. I hate playing nice." She pouted at him. He shrugged as well as a man tied spread-eagle to a four-poster bed could shrug.

"You still have your nightgown on," Nico said. "You can't get much crueler than that. Then again, my cock's inside you. If this is mean, I'd love to see vicious."

"I'll show you vicious," she said, glaring at him. She clenched her vaginal muscles as tight as she could around his cock. She did it entirely without warning, and Nico's back arched off the bed and he made a sound so sexy she wished she'd been recording him.

"Vicious." He sighed in bliss.

Enough playing. If she didn't come in the next five minutes, she refused to be held responsible for her actions. She bent low and braced herself on her forearms and rested her stomach on Nico's. She kissed his chest, his nipples, and his stomach as she moved on him.

She was close to coming, very close. Nico brought out the dominant in her like no man ever had. It made her wild to have a boy so beautiful under her, beneath her in nearly every sense of the word. He'd follow any order she gave him. He'd serve her until his dying breath if she demanded it. He'd deny himself food and water and air at her command if that was her whim. The responsibility of ownership was enormous, the pleasures endless. If Søren felt for her a fraction of what she felt for Nico, she was a well-loved woman indeed.

Nora's heart beat hard against her lungs. The room was a sauna. She sat up again and slipped her hand under the lace-edge of her gown and pressed her fingers into her swollen clitoris. She saw Nico watching as she stroked herself in time with each thrust of her hips against him. Arousal rolled like a wave through her. Nico pumped his cock up and into her. She stroked and rocked, rocked and stroked. Her eyes closed and her head fell back as she pushed, pushed, pushed against the hardness that filled her and filled her and filled her.

In the distance, she heard Nico make a sound, a soft sort of desperate grunt. Who knew why, but that's what did it for her, that small hungry groan of his.

She forgot about the Kiss, forgot about the game, forgot about anything and everything but the need to come.

She dropped her chin to her chest. Her hair fell in her face. Her entire being was centered on the aching core of her where Nico lived right now. She dug her fingernails into the tender skin of his stomach and came with a hoarse cry. Her vagina pulsed around him, tight contractions that radiated from her clitoris to her hips, up her back and down her thighs.

When the last flutter faded, Nora opened her eyes and blinked. "I needed that."

"I guess you did," he said.

"Did you come?" she asked.

"No. But it hurt not to."

Nora laughed, a happy drunken sound even to her own ears. "You didn't drop the Kiss," she said. She picked it up by the little paper flag and shook it as if it were a tiny silver bell.

"Does that mean I can come? Please?"

"I guess it does," she said, casually—and very slowly—unwrapping the chocolate. "I mean, fair is fair."

"Now?" he asked.

She waved her hand "Give me a minute. I'm hungry."

"I'm inside you."

"I can eat with a cock inside me. It's called multi-tasking."

She popped the candy in her mouth and moaned dramatically as if it were the finest gourmet chocolate in the world, and not the sort of Halloween candy one bought at the drugstore on the corner for three bucks a bag.

"Nora?" Nico said softly.

"Hmm?" She pretended to just notice he was still there.

"Please?"

She heaved a sigh. "Fine. Would you like me to untie you?"

"*S'il vous plait, Madame.*"

Nora bent forward and accidentally on purpose brushed her breasts against his face as she loosened the knot on the cord that bound his cuffs to the bedposts.

She slid off him entirely to untie his ankles. As soon as he was free of the ropes he stretched like a cat and then, quick as a cat, he rolled over and onto his hands and knees.

"Where would you like me?" Nora asked him. "On my back?"

"Right as you are," he said.

She too was on her hands and knees, by the last bedpost that still sported a length of black rope hanging off of it. Nico mounted her from behind and entered her with a rough thrust. Wet and open as she was, it didn't hurt and she certainly didn't begrudge it. He must have been dying to come by now.

There was a mirror on top of the bedroom's dresser, where she could watch him as he fucked her. He was lovely to watch. He rose up on his knees and she stared into the mirror at the sight of his cock, so thick and hard and wet, slipping in and out of her body. He was watching, too, but not in the mirror. He was looking down at where they were joined. His hands held her by the hips and Nora let him move her as he pleased.

And he pleased to move her hard against him. Nico could make love more tenderly than almost any man she'd ever been with in her life...but that's not was this was. He fucked her, that rough rutting sort of fucking that long-distance lovers knew all too well. There was an edge of anger to it, since it couldn't be like this all the time. But a touch of bliss as well, because at least it was like this now.

The room was silent but for his ragged breathing and the sound of his thick cock pounding into her wet hole. His every muscle was taut. She saw the veins in his hands and forearms popping. His need was beautiful and aroused her all over again. She rocked back against him as hard as he slammed into her.

It was primal.

It was painful.

It was perfect.

Nora came when he came, not as hard as her first orgasm, but sweeter as Nico filled her with his semen, so much of it that a few drops fell out of her between his last thrusts and landed on the antique Amish bedspread.

Oops.

She knew she'd forgotten something.

CHAPTER FIVE

"Are you going to do that all night?" Nora asked.

Nico nodded.

"I thought so," she said. "I do have wine."

Nico shrugged.

"Later. Got it," she said.

Nico had nodded and shrugged because his lips and tongue were otherwise engaged with her nipples. After defiling the bedspread, they'd curled up together in bed, and Nico had pulled the straps of her gown down—without asking first, wicked boy—and had spent now...Nora checked the mantel clock over the fireplace...seven minutes sucking her breasts.

"I should have brought a book to read," she said at eight minutes. "Wonder if I could reach my phone..."

She stretched her arm past Nico's shoulder.

No, she couldn't reach her phone. Too bad. She could have answered a few more e-mails. She ran her fingers through his soft hair, rubbed his neck and shoulders...

Nine minutes.

"I mean, don't get me wrong, Moosh," Nora said. "It does feel good. It's just..." She glanced at the clock again. "Nine minutes?"

"You've sucked me for longer than nine minutes," he said, coming up for air.

"Entirely different situation and you know it."

He shook his head and returned to his task. Nora and Nico lay on their sides, arms and legs intertwined, Nora's chin at Nico's forehead, his head buried against her chest.

Ten minutes.

"This has got to be pathological. Were you bottle-fed as a baby?" she asked. "Never mind. That was mean. I'm childless. I have no room to judge."

Twelve minutes. She was starting to get a little sore. Aroused, but sore.

"Guess it could be worse," she said with a sigh. "If you're going to have an orally-fixated boyfriend, better tits than cigarettes, right?"

Finally, Nico laughed hard enough that

Nora was able to pull away from him and yank her nightgown back into place. The boy was insatiable sometimes.

Nico reached for her and she batted his hand away.

"No, bad Moosh. It's wine o'clock."

"I have wine every day of my life," he said. "I only get your breasts four months a year."

"But it's California chardonnay," she said. "And I have more candy."

"Hmm," he said. "If there's candy…"

He pulled on his jeans and went downstairs to hunt up wine glasses while Nora opened the bottle.

He returned, triumphant with two white wine glasses just in time to catch Nora nosing through his weekender bag.

"Looking for something?" he asked as he set the wine glasses on the side table by the sofa. He picked up the wine bottle, looked at the label, and grinned.

"My present," Nora said, still nosing. She had no shame about getting caught digging through his things. She owned him all the time. While they were together she owned him even more. That meant his body was her body, his heart her heart, and his luggage her luggage. So she figured anyway.

"It's in there," he said. "Bottom."

"Is this it?" she asked, pulling out a flat white box with a black ribbon around it.

"No, that's for his birthday."

"Kingsley's?" Nora asked. Kingsley's birthday was November second, the day after she'd get back to New Orleans.

"Yeah," Nico said. "Although...ah, I don't know if I should give it to him or not."

"You should give him a present. It'll mean the world to him." Nora wanted Nico and Kingsley to have a good relationship almost as much as she wanted Nico and her to have a good relationship.

"It's not that," Nico said. "I don't know if it's the right thing to give him. He might..." Nico shrugged. His grandmother called him Moosh for a reason. Unlike nearly everyone else she knew—herself included—when Nico didn't know what to say, he said nothing.

"Can I look?" she asked.

Nico pointed at the box with his wine glass as if to say, *If you wish.*

She wished.

She slid the black ribbon off the box. It was a pretty box with a pretty bow, which likely meant Nico's cousin, the winery's office manager Marbella, had done the wrapping. She lifted the lid and found a small book, black leather.

"Photo album?" Nora guessed. Nico said nothing, so she knew she'd guessed right. He wasn't looking at her while she opened the cover to the first photograph, but focused instead on the golden liquid in his wine glass.

"Oh my God," Nora said, clapping a hand over her heart. "Look how cute you are." The photograph was of Nico—she'd know those eyes anywhere—at about age five. He was sitting on a tree stump on the edge of the winery with the house in the background. He'd caught a cricket or grasshopper or something and held it out to the camera in his palm. He was smiling and Nora saw he was missing his two front teeth.

"There's more," Nico said. "All me from five to twelve."

Nora flipped through the photo album slowly, and found her eyes were welling up. It didn't mean that much to her to see Nico as a little boy. It didn't mean that much to her to see pictures of herself as a child either. But the thoughtfulness of giving Kingsley a whole album of photos of his son, of the years Kingsley had missed...

There was Nico in shorts and a t-shirt, running from one of his other cousins, a soccer ball at his toes. There was Nico on the beach, the French Riviera, wearing his mother's too-large sunglasses with white sunblock on his nose. There was Nico, curled in a ball sleeping on a pile of clean laundry like a house cat.

"Kingsley will never recover from this," Nora said, grinning. "If the house catches on fire, he'll save Juliette, Céleste, and this photo album."

"Not Søren?" Nico asked.

"Søren will save Kingsley," Nora said.

"And what about you?"

"Who do you think set the fire?"

Nico laughed as Nora flipped through the album again.

"No baby pictures?" she asked.

He winced. "I couldn't find any."

"You have to have baby pictures somewhere."

"I mean, I couldn't find any that were me alone. Maman is the photographer, so in all the baby pictures...you know..." He fell silent again. Nora understood then. All the pictures of Nico as a baby, his father was holding him.

"You sure it's okay to give it to him?" Nico asked. "He won't be..."

"*Triste*?" Nora supplied the French word for *sad*.

"Hurt," Nico said.

"He missed twenty-five years of your life.

Of course he'll be hurt. But if there's one thing you're ever going to learn from being with me, it's that there's good pain and bad pain." She closed the photo album and held it briefly to her heart. "This is good pain."

"You can take it to him then," he said. "And tell him *bon anniversaire.*"

"He'll be touched you were worried about hurting him. He wants you to love him as much as he loves you."

"In time," he said. "Maybe." Nora understood his reticence to really let go and love Kingsley. The man who'd raised him from birth until his death two years ago still held the high ground in Nico's heart. Slowly but surely, Kingsley was making inroads. Impossible not to. Kingsley could be damn lovable when he wanted to be.

"Kingsley is the reason we're together," Nora reminded Nico.

He lifted his wine glass in a salute. "No," Nico said. He pointed at her. "You are the reason he and I are together."

"You play so hard to get," Nora said. "But this is proof you do love him. These aren't copies. These pictures are originals."

Nico shrugged, but didn't deny it.

"Okay, enough about him...where's my

present?" Nora asked. She put the box away in her bag to give to Kingsley.

"Small red box."

"Small red box," she said, digging in Nico's bag again. She found it stuffed under a pair of socks, neatly folded. "Can I open it? I don't care if you say no, I'm opening it anyway."

"Open it," he said.

Nora ripped the ribbon off the box and lifted the lid and found inside...

"Nothing?" She held up the empty box. "Or is there a very tiny diamond in here I'm just not seeing?"

Nico was a born male submissive and any male submissive worth his salt brought gifts to his mistress. She knew dominatrices who posted wishlists on their websites just so their clients would know what sort of tribute they expected. Nora had never gone that far, but she never turned down a thoughtful gift given in the right spirit. And Nico... There hadn't been one visit, one trip, one night together when he hadn't brought her something. Their first time together had been the best gift: He'd given her his company during the hardest night of her life.

Nico grinned. "It's whatever you want it to be," he said. "You tell me."

"I tell you?"

"You want to do something to me that I'm not..." He waved his hand at her, indicating he wanted her to finish his sentence for him.

"I see. You're giving me permission to do something to you."

"That's it."

"So I can use this for...pegging?"

Nico blinked, but recovered quickly. "As I said, it's whatever you want."

"Blood-play?"

He held up his hands in surrender.

"Making you get a cock piercing?"

He winced so hard both eyes closed. Slowly one eye inched open. "If you want," he said.

"Oh..." Nora said, her voice a purr. "Good present. But you know I could make you do any of that if I wanted to any old time."

"You can," he admitted. "But...I was thinking of when you were teaching me about us, about what couples like us are supposed to be like. You said real submission isn't something taken but something freely given and freely accepted."

"I said that?"

"Last year, during my, ah...training."

"God damn, I'm smart," she said.

He laughed. "Very. That's my gift. I'm

giving you my submission, and I want you to accept it from me."

"Thank you," she said, walking over to kiss him. "I do accept this beautiful gift of your submission, and you are going to regret ever giving it to me."

"No regrets yet."

"The night is still young."

They kissed a good long kiss, a wine-flavored kiss, better than candy.

"You aren't really going to make me get a piercing, are you?" he asked.

"Oh, maybe just a little one."

He took a ragged breath. "More wine, please?"

CHAPTER SIX

It didn't take long for Nico to want to make love again. (The lube Nora bought earlier came in handy for the particular act he was in the mood for.) After a quick shower together, Nico declared that he'd rather go for a walk than try to sleep just yet. Nora had taken a nap earlier to prepare for a long night. A night walk with her boyfriend at her side sounded pretty damn good to her, too.

They dressed warmly, both of them in jackets, scarves, jeans, and boots. As soon as they left the house and stepped into the night air, Nora took a deep breath and smiled. New England autumn. There was nothing like it. She inhaled deeply again, taking in chimney smoke, crisp cold air, and the sweet rot of raked leaves left to molder.

"I love that smile," Nico said as they

headed down the sidewalk. He put his arm around her waist, a possessive protective gesture she had no objections to.

"I was smiling thinking about all the possibilities of the gift you gave me. So many sadistic things I can do to you..."

Nico exhaled heavily. "Next time you're getting jewelry."

"Too late now. But speaking of smiles..."

"What?" he asked.

"When you poured the wine earlier, you smiled when you saw the label, like you were about to laugh at something. What was it?"

"Ah, you noticed." He looked sheepish, like she'd caught him cheating at cards.

"I noticed. I notice everything about you," she said, playfully elbowing him in the side.

"You bought Six Hills chardonnay. I know that winery," he said. "I worked there one summer a few years ago."

"The guy at the store said it was his favorite. Yours too?"

He shrugged. "Good wine, but, ah...I might have been involved with the owner's daughter."

Nora laughed. "Nico, did you have sex with the wine we're drinking?"

"Not with it...*near* it," he said, laughing that quiet way he had.

"How old was she?" This was a fun question Nora loved asking about Nico's exes. All the women he'd been involved with since he was seventeen were significantly older than him.

"I was twenty-two. She was...forty? Forty-two? It wasn't serious."

"I'm not jealous," Nora said. "It's okay to have exes. Neither one of us were virgins."

"My last girlfriend was jealous. It's good you aren't."

"It's even better you aren't," she said with a wink.

"How is he?" Nico asked. This was an approved question that didn't break the separation of church and state rule. *How is he?* was fine. *How is he in bed?* was not.

"He's irritated. He's in Petaluma now for a conference he'd rather not attend. Otherwise he's fine. Kingsley's good. Juliette and Céleste send their love. Michael and Griffin just got engaged, which is exciting. Oh, and I had very good sex half an hour ago with my beautiful boyfriend. Safe to say we are all doing well. And you?"

He smiled. "I'm in Halloween-ville," Nico said. "Of course I'm good."

Nora glanced around the street. Nico was right. This was Halloween-ville. Their B&B

was in a residential neighborhood that did Halloween to the nines. Nearly every house they passed had a pumpkin on the porch with an electric votive candle inside, making it look like little orange monsters were grinning and glaring at them from all around. Spiderwebs holding enormous plastic spiders hung from trees and black and orange crepe paper fluttered across doorways and porch railings. Skeletons dangled in windows. Witches with red eyes glared from rooftops. Zombie arms reached through the posts of white picket fences.

"It's just like the movies," Nico said, giddy as a schoolboy. She knew what he meant. The houses were classic New England cottages and Colonials. As they walked, red and gold leaves blew across the quiet street.

"I hope it's not a slasher flick," Nora said. "The horny girls always die first in those movies. I've got a target on my back the size of a barn."

"I'll protect you and all the horny girls of the world," Nico said. "You should watch more French films. We love horny girls. I know I do."

"That's it," Nora said. Horny girls. Yes. Perfect.

"What's it?"

Nora leaned back against a white picket fence and faced Nico. "I know how I want to use my present you gave me."

"What is it?" he asked, trying to look unconcerned though his eyes betrayed him.

"I want to watch you with another woman."

From the look of shock on his face, Nora could tell that was the last thing Nico had been expecting her to do with his "gift."

"Watch me? How?"

"Have sex," Nora said. She thought that was obvious.

"Are you serious?" he asked. He wasn't smiling anymore.

"Of course," she said. "Why not?"

"When I said I was glad you weren't the jealous type, I meant, I'm glad you don't hate how much I have to work or hate when I mention ex-girlfriends. I never thought you might…"

He paused and exhaled hard. He'd stopped talking and didn't seem like he was going to start again anytime soon. Nora filled the silence.

"I would never *make* you do it," she said. "If you don't want to, obviously you don't have to. But if you're open to it…"

"I'm not…" Nico took a long breath again.

He wasn't having an easy time with this conversation.

"Not interested?" Nora asked. "Not into it? Not that kinky? Not ready?"

"Not him," Nico said. His face was a blank mask, emotionless, but his eyes flashed with turmoil.

"Nico, I know you're not Kingsley."

"Do you?" he asked.

"Yes, I do, as a matter of fact," she said. "You wear the same size shoe. You stand the same way. You shrug the same. And you have the same nose and jawline, which is why anyone who sees you two can tell you're related. But you couldn't be more different."

"I don't sleep around with every woman—or man—on earth," he said.

"Neither does Kingsley," Nora said. She paused, rethinking the truth of that statement. "Well, not anymore anyway. And you can't judge him without judging me. I've had a lot of lovers, too. And sometimes several at once."

"I don't judge. It's not that," he said. "I'm yours."

"I know."

"*Only* yours," he said.

That "only" stung a little. She wondered if

he felt like she was foisting him off on someone else.

Nico said no more. He'd closed down to her, his arms crossed over his chest, no eye contact.

"I know you aren't Kingsley," she said again. "But I am me. And I am sort of slightly very, *very* kinky. We're still getting to know each other. You should know this is something I like to do, even if we never do it together."

Slowly he nodded. Slowly he met her eyes again. Slowly, he uncrossed his arms, stood up straight, and they set off walking again. Slowly.

"Maybe if I knew why you liked it?" Nico said.

"I don't know," she said. "Why do you like older women? You just do. It's your taste. I like kink. I like playing with others. I like watching. I like helping. My favorite sessions with clients are the ones with married couples. The husband and I dominate his wife together. It's sexy and fun and...well, that's it. It's sexy and fun. And it wouldn't have to be full-on sex. Just a blowjob would make my day."

Nico shook his head but she could see the first hint of a smile on his face. "You are..."

"Insane?" she said.

"Interesting." He paused. "And a little insane."

"Comes with the territory."

She knew he'd come to terms with her request when he slid his arm around her waist again as they walked.

"I'm not saying no to it," he said as they turned a corner. Nora knew they were close to the bay. Here the autumn smells mixed with saltwater in her nose. "I wouldn't say no to anything you really wanted."

"Then what are you saying?"

"I'm saying...how does that happen?"

"What?"

"How do you find someone to do that?" he asked. "You can't just ask someone to come over and blow your boyfriend, can you?"

"I can," she said. "But I know some interesting people back home."

"We're not at home," he said. "Do you know anyone in this town?"

"No," she said. "But I could still find a girl to play with. Easy."

"Easy?"

"Easy," she said. "If we're talking about finding a girl to fool around with you while I watch? Easy as pie."

"I don't know about that," Nico said.

"I can prove it if you let me."

"What if I don't like her?" Nico asked, shrugging. "What if she's your type but not mine?"

"I would never inflict a woman on you who you weren't excited to be with. We'll just find Salem's finest retirement community."

Nico slapped her ass. "I like younger women, too," he said.

"Liar. You do not."

"I've never been with a woman my age, but sometimes I find them attractive. I choose to be with older women because I like that they have experience and their own lives and jobs."

"So you're saying for a fling, I can find us a horny twenty-something?"

"If she wants to be with me..."

"Nico, you're twenty-six, French, and you own your own winery. You're also sexy as hell. This is not going to be a challenge."

"I think it's going to be a challenge."

"So are you saying yes? You'll do it?" Nora asked.

"If I like her too," he said again. "And if it happens naturally. Don't try to make it happen. She has to like us and we have to like her. Okay?"

"I accept those terms," Nora said. She held

out her hand to shake and Nico took it like it was a snake about to bite him. Then he wrapped his fingers around hers and pulled her roughly to him for a long kiss.

"You," he said, "could talk me into anything."

"Don't say things like that," Nora said. "Because I will."

He released her and Nora turned them down a side street.

"Where are we going?" Nico asked. Up ahead was a bright streetlight, the kind that marked commercial areas.

"To find us a girl."

Nico made a sound Nora had only ever heard Frenchmen make—a soft groan of exasperation mixed with frustration and a soupçon of utter disbelief. Nora found it adorable. She didn't tell Nico that.

"There's a couple of very nice hotels up this way," Nora said. "We would have stayed at one, but they were all booked for Halloween. We'll go into the hotel bar and hang out and if a cute lonely girl shows up, we'll invite her to our table. Eleven o'clock is prime cute-girl hunting time."

"My girlfriend wants to watch another girl suck me off. This is not what I had in mind for Halloween," he said.

"Kinky Halloween is different from Vanilla Halloween," Nora said. "I should have warned you."

"Hmm," was all he said to that, followed soon by a second "Hmm."

"Here's the thing, Moosh. You're very sexy when you're fucking. I like to look at you when you're fucking. You're usually pretty guarded, but you're not so guarded—"

"When I'm fucking, yes."

"But...when you're fucking, I'm being fucked. Hard to concentrate on the show when I'm part of the show. Understand?"

He made that sound again.

"It is a power trip, too," she admitted. "Giving a woman the order to pleasure you? Ordering you to let her?" Nora leaned against a light pole and put the back of her hand on her forehead. "Be still my horny heart." She stood up and turned around. "Oh..."

"What?" Nico asked. Nora pointed at a green sign nailed to a telephone pole.

"It says the cemetery's down that way," she said, pointing down a side street. "You want to see if we can find a ghost before we find a girl?"

"I would much rather go ghost-hunting than girl-hunting."

"Ghosts first," she said. "Girls after."

As they walked to the cemetery down the block, Nora explained to Nico who they were looking for. The Smiling Girl, dead a decade, according to their B&B owner. Very pretty. Went to meet her boyfriend for a tryst, got her throat slit instead.

"And," Nora continued, "supposedly she'll walk next to you if you're stupid enough to stroll through the graveyard at midnight."

"It's eleven," Nico said.

"Maybe she's up early."

They stood at the edge of the cemetery next to the iron gate, slightly ajar. Red maples lined the stone fence, their heavy branches swaying in the wind and dropping scarlet leaves around them. Inside the cemetery, Nora spied row after row after row of gothic-looking tombstones.

"Looks kind of spooky in there," Nora said.

"It's a cemetery," Nico said. "What is it supposed to look like? Cheerful?"

"Good point."

Hand in hand they entered the cemetery. They stayed on the main path and walked slowly through the graveyard. It wasn't large —merely one city block—but it was one of the creepier cemeteries Nora had ever visited. Considering she lived near one of New Orleans's famous crypt yards, that was saying something.

The headstones were so old and weathered that she could barely read the names on them. The trees were overgrown and let in little light from the surrounding streets. She and Nico walked very close to each other, holding hands, and didn't stray from the path. She wasn't scared of hands reaching out of the ground or ghosts or demons, but in a cemetery this old and neglected, there was a good chance there were rocks or divots or branches just waiting to break the ankles of unsuspecting tourists.

"What do you think?" Nora asked.

"It's beautiful," Nico said.

She knew exactly what he meant. It did look like something off a vintage Halloween postcard.

"Do you ever think about where you're going to be buried?" Nico asked.

"That's such a French question."

Nico laughed softly. "I want to be buried in my vines," he said. "So my body can nourish them."

"Too bad. Kingsley already bought a family crypt in New Orleans. You have a shelf."

"I have a shelf?"

"It's under my shelf."

"You'll be on top of me for eternity?"

Nora nodded.

"I can live with that. No, not *live* with it…"

Nora laughed and put her arm through Nico's. They'd made it halfway along the main path and were nearing the bend in the U that would, she assumed, lead them back to the front gates.

"You see any ghosts?" Nora asked.

"Not a one," Nico said. "You?"

"No."

"I don't see any either," said a woman from behind them.

CHAPTER EIGHT

Nora screamed and Nico spun around so fast his boots sent gravel flying everywhere.

"Oh, oh...sorry. Didn't mean to scare you."

The woman apologizing was about Nico's age, wearing an off-the-rack sexy witch costume that showed ample bare flesh. The tip of the pointed hat on her head was rakishly tilted to one side, and she was holding onto her broom with both hands.

"You're dressed as a witch and you're in a cemetery at night sneaking up on people," Nora said, still panting. "Are you sure you didn't mean to scare us?"

The girl cringed, winced, and squirmed in her shoes all at once.

"I really didn't mean to," she said in a small

voice. "I was just cutting through the cemetery. It's on my way home from work."

"Where do you work?" Nora asked. "A nightmare factory?"

"Two Keys Tavern, down the dock," she said. "I'm a bartender. We all dress in costumes during October. This was about the last outfit left at the costume shop. It was either slutty witch or slutty nurse. Or slutty nun, which I didn't know was a thing."

"It's a thing," Nora said.

The woman had a light Boston accent so that *dock* sounded like "dahck" and *bartender* came out "bahr-tendah."

"There's always next Halloween," the slutty witch said. "I'm Justine, by the way. Sorry again for scaring you."

"Justine?" Nora said. "Like the Marquis de Sade novel?"

"No…like Justine Bateman from the TV show *Family Ties*," the girl said, narrowing her eyes at Nora. "But now we know something about you we didn't know before."

"I knew," Nico said. The girl, Justine, laughed. It was good laugh. Good laugh for a cute girl. Very cute. She had laughing eyes and a sweet face and hair the color of apple cider. And the slutty witch outfit was definitely working for her.

"I'm Nora, by the way. This is my Nico."

"Nice to meet you, Justine," Nico said, shaking her hand.

"Ah, good accent. Is that...Italian?" Justine asked.

"French," he said.

"Better accent than mine," Justine said, grinning. "So I guess that answers my question. You two aren't from around here?"

"New Orleans," Nora said. "And a vineyard in the south of France. Just here for Halloween. We were ghost-hunting the Smiling Girl."

"Waste of time," Justine said. "I've been in this graveyard a million times. Never seen her. And I know every dead person in this place. Hey, can I give you a cemetery tour? I owe you after scaring the shit out of you both."

Nico nodded. "Sure," Nora said, incapable of saying no to cute girls dressed as slutty witches. "Lead the way."

With her broom, Justine pointed down the path. "Follow me...into hell," she said in a dramatic voice.

Justine started off, and Nora and Nico fell in step right behind her.

"Welcome to St. Patrick's Cemetery," she intoned in a bland tour guide voice. "Established in 1796 at the edge of town in response to a cholera outbreak. We had more bodies than holes to put them in. Oh yes, people were puking and shitting themselves to death back then. Do you ever wish time travel were real? Well, don't. Nobody but fucking idiots would go back in time."

"Is this part of the official cemetery tour?" Nico asked Justine.

"I'm a little off the script," Justine said. "Carrying on." She pointed with her broom at a large headstone on her right. "Here lies General Robert McMahon of Revolutionary War fame. Hero. Legend. Total asshole."

"You think so?" Nico asked.

"Well, yeah, his wife is buried on the other side of the cemetery, and she died after him, so...you put two and two together, you get an asshole."

"Those numbers add up for me," Nora said.

"And over here," Justine said, doing a little twirl wherein she tossed her broom in an arc to point at another grave, "lies Elizabeth Dunne, famous for maybe having boinked Nathanial Hawthorne."

"She boinked Nathanial Hawthorne?" Nora asked.

"What's boinking?" Nico asked.

"What we were doing half an hour ago," Nora said.

"Ah," Nico replied. "Boinking."

Nora loved teaching him English slang.

"According to local legend," Justine said, still employing her tour guide voice, "she owned an inn he frequented, and she was reputed to be very attractive. And something of an ass freak."

"He got a piece of her scarlet A," Nora said.

"A whole lot of scarlet A," Justine said, nodding. "But no judgment here. I've been known to enjoy a little scarlet A myself every now and then."

Nora started to follow her but Nico stopped her with a hand on Nora's arm.

"I like her," Nico said, *soto vocce*.

Nora pinched his cheeks. "I'm so proud of my boy."

"You two coming?" Justine asked. "So many assholes, so little time."

"Story of my life," Nora said.

The impromptu tour lasted another twenty minutes. It wasn't a very big cemetery, though—according to Justine—it had more than its fair share of assholes and ass freaks.

"And that concludes our stroll through St. Patrick's," Justine said with a little curtsey.

Nora and Nico golf-clapped.

"Thank you," Nora said. "You were a fabulous tour guide. I'm glad to know that so many early settlers were...what did you call them?"

"The Salem Bitches," Justine said.

"Right," Nora said.

"So, yeah, really sorry about scaring the bejesus out of you two earlier," Justine said, smiling impishly.

"Are you?" Nora asked.

"Hmm...I admit I kind of did it on purpose. Hate all the fucking tourists we have to deal with in October, but if I'd known you two were so adorable, I might not have done it," Justine said.

"We are pretty adorable," Nora said. "Want to go get a drink somewhere? I'm buying."

Justine grinned broadly but the smile faded when she glanced down at her phone. "Ah, shit. I'd love to, but I gotta get home. I'm working the morning shift."

"At a bar?" Nora asked. "This is a rough town."

Justine smiled. "Taking my grandma to her hair appointment. Why do old people get up so early? And really, she's ninety. Who's she trying to impress?"

"Nico," Nora said, causing him to smack her on the ass again.

Justine raised an eyebrow.

"She teases me because I like older women," Nico explained.

"I've got eleven years on him," Nora said.

"Now I'm kind of sad I'm only twenty-eight," Justine said, a twinkle in her eyes. Nico brought out that twinkle in a lot of ladies.

"That's two years older than me," Nico said, wearing a sly smile to match her twinkle. "It counts."

"Is he flirting with me?" Justine asked Nora.

"If he knows what's good for him, he is," Nora said.

Justine pointed her broom at them. "I like you two. You're good people."

"We're going to a costume party tomorrow night at the Highbury. You want to be our date?"

"That sounds amazing. But...I wouldn't be a third wheel?" Justine asked. She looked eager but nervous. She'd probably never gone on a date with a couple before.

"If you're a tricycle, you need a third wheel," Nora said. "We'd love to hang out with you more."

"You twisted my arm," Justine said. "I'm in."

They exchanged numbers. Nora hugged Justine, and Nico kissed both her cheeks goodnight. Justine took great delight in having a Frenchman kiss her in the classic *bise-bise* French style.

Nora and Nico watched Justine stroll off to her apartment. Just before she disappeared out of sight, she turned and blew them both a kiss.

"I told you it wouldn't be hard," Nora said.

Nico slowly shook his head in wonder and said one word:

"Rembrandt."

CHAPTER NINE

Nora and Nico slept obscenely late the next morning. They had sex upon waking, went back to sleep, and almost had sex again upon waking the second time, but decided they needed food more than sex. By then they'd missed breakfast at the B&B, but a large brunch at the Ugly Mug diner saved them from cannibalism.

Nora and Nico texted back and forth with Justine all day. She gave them suggestions galore of places to visit. Through their texting, they learned Justine was bartending by night to pay for her master's in Art Education by day. Justine thought it was "amazing" that Nico, barely twenty-six, had his own winery in France and begged to try some of his wine if it were for sale in Salem. She thought it was equally "amazing" that Nora was a published author. Nora promised her wine and dirty books, and Justine said if they weren't careful, she'd tie them up in her basement and never let them leave Salem.

This, Justine texted, was how people flirted in Salem.

Nora approved.

Soon as the sun set at the ungodly early hour of six in the evening, Nora and Nico headed out on foot to a nearby haunted museum attraction Justine had recommended. Hand in hand, they wandered long dark hallways where zombies, ghosts, and demons awaited them around every corner and behind every door. In a room labelled "The Oddities," a collection of medical nightmares that had been discovered in the home of a doctor six decades earlier were on display. Nora and Nico peered through the glass at deformed animals stuffed and mounted, tumors with hair, and even one human brain preserved in formaldehyde.

"This is so disgusting," Nora said, wincing at the sight of a tapeworm in a jar. It was one hundred feet long and had been supposedly removed from a woman's stomach in 1898. Proof Justine was right that time travel was for idiots.

"Eh, it's not so bad," Nico said.

"The woman thought she was pregnant for two years, and it wasn't a baby. It was a tapeworm."

Nico shrugged. "In France, that's like a...like a kid's book. You know, a secret pet."

Nora narrowed her eyes at him. "What happened to the French to make you all like this? Was it the Revolution? It was, wasn't it?"

They survived the haunted house. Nora screamed and jumped twice, Nico once. In Nico's defense, he screamed because Nora stepped on his foot. In Nora's defense, she only stepped on his foot because a young girl in a torn and bloodstained nightgown and white facepaint reached out from under a table and grabbed her ankle with a claw-like hand.

Nico held Nora tightly and patted her back while she caught her breath.

"That was a demon," she said. "A demon attacked me."

"It was only a baby demon."

"Next time you want to celebrate an American holiday, we're celebrating mother-fucking Thanksgiving."

"You're so cute when you're terrified," Nico said into her ear.

"I think I pissed myself."

"Maybe not so cute."

Thankfully, Nora did not piss herself, and Nico's foot was fine. He'd been wise to wear his steel-toed work boots this evening.

Once Nora recovered from her brush with the demonic ghost girl, she was more than ready for dinner. Afterward, she and Nico picked separate rooms to get ready in for the costume party at the Highbury. She didn't have to do much but shimmy into her cheerleader outfit and put her hair into pigtails. Nico's costume, whatever it was, took a little longer. They were meeting Justine in front of the Highbury at nine and it wasn't until 8:30 that Nico called out from the bathroom.

"Ready?"

"I've been ready for an hour, pretty boy. You're the one taking forever."

"I can take forever," Nico said. "I have all the time in the world."

He emerged from the bathroom. He had changed into black breeches and Hessian boots, a silk vest, white shirt with an elaborate cravat, and a black and silver silk jacket very much in the classic Georgian style. He looked dashing. And a little familiar.

Nora crossed her arms and tapped her foot on the floor. "Didn't I tell you not to dress like Kingsley?"

"I didn't," Nico said.

He smiled to bare his fangs.

Nora nearly screamed again. "Oh my God."

"You told me *Interview with the Vampire* was one of your favorite books."

"And movies," she said. "Holy...you look amazing. Can I call you Lestat? "

"I'm yours. You can call me whatever you want," he said.

He held out his hand and she slowly slipped her fingers into his. With a quick jerk he pulled her to him, spun her so that her back rested against his chest, and dug his quite realistic fangs into her jugular vein.

"Oh...it tickles," she said, half-laughing, half-purring. "I like it. Do you have any fake blood on you?"

He did. Nora took it and applied it to her neck.

"Now I'm a cheerleader for the damned," she said.

"And a very sexy one," Nico said. He was standing behind her at the mirror while she applied the fake blood. His hands kept wandering under her short skirt.

"Save that for Justine."

"I have two hands. I can grope you both."

Nora kissed him. "Such a good boy."

On the cab ride to the hotel, Nico was quiet, more so than usual. Nora took his hand in hers and squeezed it.

"I take good care of my property," she said in French. "Nothing happens that you don't want to happen."

Nico said nothing, and simply kissed her. As it was a French kiss, she took it as a good sign.

The cab let them off a block from the hotel, which was as close as he could get on Halloween night in Salem, Massachusetts. Nora and Nico emerged into a carnival of costumes. She spotted two Iron Mans (Iron Men?), every possible type of witch (good, bad, and ugly), one slave Princess Leia (he must have been freezing his ass off), and two Captain Americas.

"Do you have anyone like Captain America in France?" Nora asked Nico as they worked their way through the crowd.

"Yes," he said. "Charles de Gaulle."

"Charles de Gaulle was a real person," Nora reminded him, "not a comic book hero."

Nico grinned, baring his fangs. "*Exactement.*"

She pinched his sweet undead ass for being cheeky.

They finally made it through the freak

show to the Highbury. Nora couldn't help but feel a little proud of all the admiring looks Nico received from the women they passed, and from quite a few of the men. In truth, however, she preferred the way Nico looked the other 364 days of the year, when he could be found in worn jeans and work boots, with garden shears in his hands and dirt up to his knees and elbows.

"There's Justine," Nora said, pointing at the girl coming through the crowd. It was impossible to miss her in her scarlet red witch's dress and her matching red hat.

Her orange-red hair was coiffed in old-fashioned victory rolls, and she wore glamorous ruby red lipstick. She'd dressed to impress, and Nora had a feeling Justine had dressed to impress Nico. Justine spied them and waved enthusiastically. They had to push past an adult baby, Catwoman, and a satanic surgeon with blood on his scrubs to get to her. Nora eyed the baby, the surgeon, and the woman in the cat suit.

"I feel like I'm back at The 8th Circle," she said.

Nico smiled. "You had big Halloween parties there?"

"No, this is what it looked like every night."

Justine managed to weave her way through the crush of people like she had cast a spell on them. They didn't even seem to notice her.

"This is crazy, right?" Justine asked, bright-eyed and blushing.

"A little," Nora said. "I've seen crazier. You look fabulous."

"Thank you." Justine patted her hair coquettishly. "Took me two hours to get my hair to do this. Hope it was worth it."

Nico said, "Worth every second."

Justine pointed at him and addressed Nora. "Are all Frenchmen this suave?"

"In my limited experience, yes," Nora said.

Justine turned to Nico. "What's the immigration process like in France right now?"

"A nightmare," he said.

"Hmm," Justine said. "Still gonna do it."

Nico put one arm around Nora's waist and the other around Justine's as they walked up the steps of the Highbury and through the open double doors.

Nora gave the doorman their tickets—three of them—and Justine asked, "How much do I owe you for mine?"

"It's on me," Nora said. "You're our date, remember?"

"Are you one of those rich writers?" Justine asked.

"I wish," Nora said. "I'm a decently-paid writer. But I have a second job."

"Professional cheerleader?" Justine asked.

"Dominatrix," Nico said.

Justine's brown eyes widened to saucers. "Wow," she said. "Really?"

Nora nodded.

"So you weren't kidding about the Marquis de Sade thing," Justine said.

"I read more de Sade than I watched *Family Ties*," Nora said.

"I can imagine," Justine said. "So you're a dominatrix and a writer. And he's a farmer."

"Right," Nora said.

"So...how the hell does a dominatrix from New Orleans hook up with a French farmer?"

"Do you want the long version or the short version?" Nora asked.

"Short version first," Justine said.

"I used to work for Nico's father."

"As a...writer?"

"As a dominatrix," Nora said.

Justine looked at Nico, and then back at Nora. "Yeah, I'm gonna need that long version."

CHAPTER TEN

The Highbury was an historic hotel with marble floors, red and gold Oriental rugs scattered here, there, and everywhere. Tarnished brass chandeliers cast low broken light over the partygoers. Nico fetched drinks from the bar—a beer for Justine, red wine for himself, a bourbon sour for Nora—and they all sat in a quiet-ish corner of the main lobby by the grand fireplace. Nico snagged a large armchair and Nora sat on his knee. Justine sat on the end of a long red sofa with her legs crossed, the tip of her red high heel occasionally brushing Nora's leg, occasionally brushing Nico's.

Nora gave Justine the short version of the long version of how she met Nico. Justine listened in astonished silence, her pretty red lips parted as she looked from Nora to Nico and back to Nora again.

"Well?" Nora asked.

"So...you used to work for his biological father as a dominatrix in New York. Then someone told you there was a guy in France who was probably his son that he didn't know about, and you went and found him?"

"Right," Nora said. "Confused?"

"Skeptical," Justine said, her eyes narrowed. "Are you shitting me?"

Nora shook her head.

"It *is* Halloween," Justine reminded her. "People pull tricks on each other. Hence the phrase...trick or treat? I think we're all familiar with that saying?"

"Vaguely," Nora said. Nico merely laughed. "But it's all true. I've known Nico's biological father since I was sixteen. He helped keep me out of juvie."

"And this is how you repay him? By boinking his son?"

"It's my fault it happened," Nico said to Justine before Nora could answer. "She did nothing wrong."

Ah, Nico. This is why Nora loved him. Not once had Nico allowed anyone to blame her for their unorthodox relationship. His honor—and male pride—wouldn't allow it.

Nora remembered when Kingsley had come to Nico's house looking for her right after they'd started seeing each other. Nico had bodily inserted himself between her and his father. *You don't talk to her, you talk to me. You don't blame her, you blame me. You don't fight with her, you fight with me,* Nico said once, then twice, easily a hundred times, in English and in French, softly and loudly and right in Kingsley's face.

When Kingsley attempted to push past Nico to speak to Nora, the two men had almost come to blows. Nora had tried to make peace. She got two words out—*Nico, please*—before Nico had shushed her with a hiss and a slash of his hand (a gesture which Nora found equal parts chauvinistic and sexy). *Go upstairs,* Nico had ordered her. *This is between me and my father.*

Later Kingsley would tell her that was the first moment he'd had hope for him and Nico —when Nico, even in his fury, had called Kingsley his father.

"So you're saying it's true?" Justine asked Nora. "It's all Nico's fault?"

"Let's say...if he hadn't followed me across two countries, this—us—wouldn't have happened. Since the moment we met, I had this feeling—dread, specifically—that it was inevitable, but I never would have made the first move."

"I stalked her and seduced her," Nico said, utterly shameless about the whole thing, which she appreciated.

"Stalking is such a strong word," Nora said.

"I waited until you were in the bathroom, dug through your bag to see where you were staying, and I followed you there without telling you I was coming."

"Stalking might be the right word," Nora said.

"It was a few days after her mother died," Nico explained. "She'd flown to France to have dinner with me. Then she drove into Germany where she was staying alone in a cabin in the middle of nowhere. I showed up on her doorstep in a storm. She was too lonely and heartbroken to send me away, which I knew she would be."

"Evil," Justine said.

"I was already in love and willing to, ah, how do you say…?" He snapped his fingers, trying to remember. "Press my advantage?" he said, not bragging but not *not* bragging either. He had more in common with Kingsley than he was willing to admit. "Otherwise I knew she'd never let it happen, because she was so close to my father and didn't want to hurt him."

"Were you trying to hurt him?" Justine asked Nico, an astute question and one Nora had never had the guts to ask. This was a good date. They were already opening their hearts to each other. And Justine was a good listener. If Nico could open up to her, that spoke volumes about the girl.

"He accused me of it," Nico said. "Using her to hurt him, I mean. I wasn't. It had nothing to do with him at all. But I wasn't thinking of his feelings either. I would now but, ah…too late." Nico gave Nora a little smile.

"That's so wicked hot," Justine said, obviously impressed. "I wish someone would be that ruthless to get me into bed."

"It's funny," Nora said. "My mom's one wish for me was that I'd settle down with a nice young man. Someone who'd love me and never hurt me in any way. Somehow when she died, she made sure that happened."

"Ghosts are matchmakers," Justine said. "You always gotta watch out for ghosts. But what about dear old dad? How's he taking it?"

"Kingsley? He's happy for us now," Nora said. "We're one big happy weird fucking family. Emphasis on the fucking."

It was true. The fight about Nico had cleared the air between her and Kingsley at last. Kingsley and Nico had a good relationship that was getting better all the time. Kingsley had Søren to himself when she was in France. She and Kingsley had been lovers, they'd been business partners, and they'd been rivals. Finally, now, at last, they were friends.

"That is wild. I'm going to need a lot more alcohol to process this." Justine lifted her empty beer glass. "Not really, but any excuse to drink, right?"

"All taken care of," Nora said. "Care to pour?"

"Of course," Nico said.

Nora hopped off his lap and unzipped her large purse she'd brought with her. From it she pulled a bottle of syrah.

"Is that yours?" Justine asked Nico.

He nodded. "One store in town sells it. We're not a very big winery."

"He's being modest," Nora said. "His Rosanella syrah has won all the major industry awards. Older vintages sell for hundreds of dollars a bottle."

"Then deal me in," Justine said.

Nora fetched wine glasses from the bar and Nico poured the Rosanella.

"I've heard of BYOB," Justine said. "But never BYOW."

"Now you have," Nico said. "Try it."

"Not yet," Nora said before Justine could lift her glass. "We have to toast."

"Oh, yeah, definitely," Justine said.

"A toast, then," Nico said, raising his glass, "to Halloween, candy, and mischief, but most of all to beautiful wine and delicious women."

"Candy is dandy," Justine said. "But liquor is quicker."

"I'll drink to that," Nora said. They all clinked their glasses and drank.

Justine moaned softly with pleasure when she lowered her glass to her knee. "I hate being broke," she said. "I'd drink this stuff every day if I had money."

"I was broke at your age, too," Nora said. "Hang in there. Your thirties are a lot more fun than your twenties."

"I don't know if that's possible. I'm having all the fun tonight," she said.

"Good," Nora said. "Want to have even more fun?"

"What did you have in mind?"

"Shall we dance?" Nora asked.

"I don't dance," Nico said.

"I wasn't talking to you, Dracula," Nora said. "Justine?"

She grinned again. "I thought you'd never ask. You going to save our seats?" she said to Nico.

"Nope," Nora said and winked at Nico. "He's going to watch."

The three of them found the small ballroom, which looked like a scene from the Monster Mash. Werewolves were dancing with zombie prom queens, Superman with Satan. A DJ dressed as Santa Claus played dance music interspersed with the occasional horror movie scream or demonic cackle.

Nora took Justine out onto the dance floor while Nico stood by the red velvet curtains with his wine in hand, watching them. The DJ put on "Love Shack" followed by a little "Crazy in Love" followed by "Thriller," which got all the werewolves howling. Justine was in the mood to put on a good show for Nico. She threw her arms around Nora's shoulders and danced as dirty as any dirty dancer has ever danced in the history of dirty dancing. There were pelvic thrusts, slinking spins, and some playful spanking. Nico simply stood, watched, and laughed at the performance.

"He's so sexy," Justine said to Nora. "And the accent kills me. If I didn't love you already, Mistress Nora, I'd hate you. If you meet another one of him, send him to me, okay?"

"You can have that one if you want," Nora said. "I'll share."

"Don't tempt me."

"It's what I do," Nora said, spinning Justine away from her and back in. "I tempt people."

It might have been the tone of Nora's voice or the look on her face that did it, but she saw the moment when Justine realized Nora was not kidding.

"You mean you'd really share him?" Justine asked. She'd stopped dancing to ask the question. She even glanced over at Nico who gave her a little wave.

"I mean it," Nora said. She pulled Justine closer to her. The girl had a lovely body and it had been too long since she'd been with a girl. Weeks even. They started slow dancing in a very silly manner to amuse their audience of one. Plus, it allowed them to have a serious talk. "I told Nico last night I wanted to watch him with another woman."

"Watch him do what? Like...are we talking lap dance? Kissing? Ass freakery?"

"Blowjob mainly," Nora said. "That's my personal fantasy."

"I would pay cold hard cash to go down on Nico," she said.

Nora laughed. "Luckily, he's free. And if you're interested, he likes you."

"He does?" she asked.

"He does. He thinks you're beautiful and funny and fun."

"I think he's beautiful and funny and fun. We have so much in common," Justine said, fluttering her hands in front of her face in excitement. "But...I don't know. I've never done this before. Well, not since college."

"If you're not interested, don't worry about it. We're just glad you wanted to hang out with us."

"Hey, hey, hey now," Justine said, glancing over at Nico again. "Don't try to talk me out of it. Try to talk me into it."

"That's not how it works. I don't push or pressure. I just open the door. Up to you to walk through."

"So the door's open?" Justine asked.

"Wide open," Nora said.

"How wide?"

"Wide as the Montana sky, beautiful. I promise. Go kiss him," Nora said.

"On the mouth?" Justine asked, putting on a very good show of being scandalized.

"For starters," Nora said with a wink.

"What about you?"

"I can kiss him whenever I want," Nora said.

"I mean, can I kiss you?"

"Have you ever kissed another woman before?" Nora asked.

"Never," Justine said. "Well, not since college."

"Just give it the old college try then."

Before their lips met, a new song came on. "Cream," by Prince & the New Power Generation. Justine cocked her head to the side and pointed at a speaker.

"That's a sign," Justine said.

"Definitely."

They kissed.

CHAPTER ELEVEN

Justine was clearly nervous so Nora took it easy on her. The kiss was nothing more than a light brushing of lips, followed by a second longer brush.

Justine pulled away, grinning. "Do you think Nico was watching?"

Nora looked over and Nico flashed her the okay sign of approval.

"He was watching," Nora said. "Now go kiss him."

Justine took a long deep breath, squared her shoulders, and straightened her hat.

"I'm going in," Justine said. "If I don't make it back in ten minutes, don't come and get me."

"Make me proud, kiddo," Nora said.

Justine strode over to where Nico stood by the velvet drapes. Nora watched, smiling, as he leaned in to hear whatever it was Justine whispered in his ear. Must have been good because he smiled and glanced Nora's way, seeking permission.

Nora waved her hand, telling him to get on with it, and then with his eyes still on hers, he kissed Justine on the mouth.

The kiss lasted no longer than Nora and Justine's had. They were all still getting to know each other. Nora walked back to them and patted Justine on her witchy little behind.

"Good girl," Nora said. Justine was bright-eyed, blushing and beaming all at once. Nora could have lit a cigarette off the heat of her face.

"I…I'm going to faint," Justine said.

"Nico, hold her," Nora said.

Nico wrapped Justine in his arms, and Justine leaned into the embrace and sighed.

"I used to complain about all the Halloween tourists," Justine said, eyes closed in her bliss. "Never again."

Nico took her chin in his hand and kissed her again. This time the kiss lasted a little bit longer.

"Now one for me," Nora said. Still holding Justine, Nico leaned in to kiss Nora. Nora stopped him with a hand on his chest. "Not you. Her."

Justine playfully pushed Nico away as if he were old news, threw her arms around Nora's shoulders, and kissed her with the longest kiss yet.

"See?" Nora asked. "That wasn't so bad, was it?"

"I think I'll survive," Justine said. "But one more just to check."

She turned to Nico for another kiss and he obliged. He obliged for a very long time. While Nora could happily watch her young lover get into mischief all night, they still had things to do.

"Come on, lustbirds," Nora said. "More of that later. Party first. Make-out later."

"What are we doing?" Justine asked as Nora took her hand. Justine took Nico's and the three of them wove their way through the horde of dancing bodies.

"This is Nico's first Halloween, and he leaves tomorrow. We need to do *all* the Halloween stuff, and we need to do it now."

"All of it?" Justine asked.

"All of it. Starting with..." Nora led them to the hotel lobby's bar where a pumpkin carving station had been set up and pumpkin beer was being served by the snifter-ful.

"Booze *and* carving knives," Justine said,

shaking her head. "What could possibly go wrong?"

For a first timer, Nico did fairly well. The face he carved on his pumpkin was a rather standard triangle-eyed ghoul, but all in all it was an excellent amateur effort. Nora carved a simple cat face into hers, complete with whiskers. Justine wowed them both with her creation. Into her pumpkin she carved a complete graveyard, with the largest tombstone bearing the letters *R.I.P.*

"That's fantastic," Nora said.

"In Salem, they teach you this shit from birth," Justine said. "If you can't carve a decent pumpkin by sixteen, they won't let you get your driver's license."

After pumpkin carving they bobbed for apples. Nora failed miserably at this task. Justine didn't do much better. Both of them simply ended up with wet faces and wet hair. Nico, however, got his apple in his first bite.

"It's the fangs," Justine said as she repaired her lipstick. "Gotta be the fangs."

"And the oral fixation," Nora said. Justine raised an eyebrow.

Once they'd all dried off from their faceplant in the apple tank, they found the hotel's fortune-teller and had their palms read.

The verdict? Nora would be coming into money soon.

"Not news," she said. "I get a royalty payment every first week of November."

Nico's fortune was that he would be going on a long journey very soon.

"Yeah," Nora said. "His flight for France leaves tomorrow at one."

As for Justine...she would face a challenge soon that would have a positive outcome.

"So that means I should have a threesome tonight?" Justine asked the fortune-teller.

The fortune-teller looked at her in surprise, then looked at Nora and Nico. "I would if I were you."

That sealed the deal.

At midnight, the party atmosphere turned from festive to drunken roar.

"Let's get out of here," Nora said. No, she didn't actually say it. She screamed it over the din of the crowd.

"My car's nearby," Justine said. "I hope."

"Nearby" on Halloween in Salem meant six blocks away, but as hot as the hotel was, the crisp night air was more than welcome.

"Did we miss anything?" Nora asked as Nico put his arm around her to keep her warm. "Costume party. Haunted house."

"Did you all trick-or-treat?" Justine asked.

"We're a little old for that," Nora said.

"Not in Salem," she said. "Hold on. I got this."

They were on a residential street. Justine ran ahead of them, racing up to porches and glancing around. Nico looked at Nora in confusion.

"Found it!" Justine called in a stage whisper. She stood on someone's front porch. All the lights were off in the house except for the half dozen pumpkins on the stoop still glowing from the electric candles inside.

Nora and Nico came up the walkway to her.

Justine held a bowl in her hand. "A lot of people leave out their leftovers," she said. "Go for it."

Nora waved Nico forward.

"Trick or treat?" he said.

"Where's your bag?" Justine asked. "Wait. I have a better idea."

She unwrapped a mini Kit-Kat and popped one end in her mouth between her teeth. Nico took the other end in his and bit it off.

Then the porch light came on.

"Shit," Justine said. All three of them ran from the house laughing like naughty children, which was exactly what they were.

They were still laughing when they reached Justine's car. Once inside and on the way back to the B&B, Justine told stories of her childhood antics in Salem on Halloween, the stunts she and her brother had pulled, the tricks they played.

"Does anyone ever choose trick?" Nico asked. "I mean, after you say, 'Trick or treat'?"

"You mean does anybody ever refuse a kid candy and roll the dice on a trick?" Justine asked.

"Right," Nico said.

"Not that I know of. Most people give up the candy. Better than getting your house egged or rolled," Justine said, and quickly explained what "rolling" was to Nico.

"Toilet paper?" Nico asked.

"They're not very good tricks," Justine said. "Pretty amateur stuff."

"If you're not going to trick someone right," Nora said, "you shouldn't trick them at all."

"I used to pull tricks on my family when I was a kid," Justine said. "They made me stop after that time I faked my own kidnapping."

"Sweetheart, that's not a trick," Nora said. "That's psychological torture. You sure you're not a secret dominatrix?"

"Not yet. Maybe after tonight," Justine

said. She winked at Nico who replied by tugging one of Justine's curls. Aww, the kids were flirting. So adorable.

Nico turned and looked at Nora in the backseat. He had a mischievous glint in his eyes. "Trick or treat?"

"Trick," she said. She did love a challenge.

"Okay," he said. "You asked for it."

CHAPTER TWELVE

They arrived at the B&B a few minutes later. The three of them left the pumpkins they'd carved on the porch with the other Halloween decorations and quietly crept up the stairs (or as quietly as three slighty-tipsy revelers could manage).

"Cool room," Justine said as she unpinned her witch's hat and dropped it on the dresser. "Thanks for having me over."

"Glad you could join us," Nora said. "Wine, Nico."

Nico nodded and poured three glasses for them all.

"That's nice," Justine said when Nico handed her the glass. "You just…give an order and he follows it? That how it works?"

Nico glanced at Nora, waiting, probably as curious to hear her answer as Justine was.

"Not quite," Nora said. "He's got a mind of his own, damn him."

"You'd never love a doormat," Nico said.

"Never," she said.

"I thought you guys like…licked boots and stuff like that? I'm sorry if that's a rude question. I'm just curious." Justine sat on the edge of the bed. Nora liked how careful she was with her wine glass, trying not to spill it even as she sat. She was respectful and mature. A good person to play with. All fun, no drama.

"Ask all the questions you want," Nora said. "That's how we learn. You gave us a history lesson about Salem. Here's one about us: There's lots of different ways to submit in a kink relationship. There are subs, submissives. There are slaves. There are service tops. Lots of options. What we do, Nico and I, it's something that began in France around the late eleventh century. It came out of the culture of courtly love—young knights would fall in love with a married lady and serve her faithfully and devotedly. It was supposed to be chaste love, but we've all seen how well that worked with Queen Guinevere and Sir Lancelot."

"He lanced her," Justine said. "A lot."

"Precisely," Nora said. "I have someone I'm practically married to who I spend most of my life with. And I have Nico who serves a very different role."

"I'm like her knight," Nico said. "In private, I please her. In public, I protect her whether it pleases her or not. If someone insults her, I defend her honor. If someone tries to hurt her, I hurt him. When we're playing, she's in charge. When it's serious, I take over."

"So no boot-licking," Justine said.

"I have clients who pay me money to lick my boots. Nico gets to lick everything else."

Justine laughed. "So if I said something really rude to the mistress over here," Justine said to Nico, "you'd kick me out?"

"I'd *escort* you out," Nico said, gesturing with his wine glass to the door. "You insult her once?" He shrugged. "You don't get to do it twice."

As opposed to Søren, Nora thought, who would likely agree with the insult. And he would probably be right.

"Okay," Justine said. "Got it. Understood. One more question though."

"Ask," Nico said, smiling at her.

"Will you marry me?"

"Tonight?" Nico asked, his eyebrows raised.

"I'm asking both of you," Justine said. "Gotta be legal somewhere, yeah?"

"Oregon," Nora said. "I assume."

"You two are awesome," Justine said, grinning.

"So are you," Nora said. "You ready to play?"

Justine took a long breath as if steeling herself. "Yeah," she said. "I think." She looked at Nico who lifted his wine glass to her in a salute. "Okay, definitely ready to play."

"Nervous?" Nora asked her.

"A....little tiny bit nervous," she said, her voice hitting a high note and squeaking.

Nico stood by the end of the bed, leaning on the post.

Nora blew a kiss at him. "Don't worry," she told Justine. "So is Nico."

"Are you?" Justine asked him.

He nodded.

"You?" Justine asked Nora, who shook her head slowly. "Because you're only watching?"

"I'm not watching," Nora said. "I'm cheer-leading."

Nora raised her arms and shook her invisible pompoms. Nico rolled his eyes.

"Plus," Nora said, collapsing into the armchair and stretching her legs out onto the ottoman, "nothing's going to happen—wait. I need my riding crop to do this speech."

She leaned over the side of the chair, unzipped her toy bag and pulled out her favorite red riding crop.

"Okay," she said, pointing her crop at Justine and Nico. "As I was saying, nothing is going to happen that you don't want to happen. Both of you. If either of you gets uncomfortable, you say 'I want to stop,' and guess what? Everything stops. Then we drink a little wine, eat a few Kit-Kats, find a bad horror movie on TV or call it a night. *Comprendnez-vous?*"

"*Je comprends parfaitement, mon amour,*" Nico said.

"Ah…French," Justine said. "Don't know what you both said. Don't care. Whatever you tell me to do to him, I'm ready and willing to do it."

"Good," Nora said. "Let's start easy. Take off his jacket for him. *S'il te plaît.*"

It was a simple order, but Nora could see Justine was still nervous as she raised her hands to Nico's buttons and slowly undid them.

"Very good," Nora said as Justine pushed the jacket off Nico's shoulders. "Now fold it and put it on the dresser."

Justine obeyed. "Next?" she asked.

"Shirt," Nora said.

"This is so crazy," Justine said as she went to work on Nico's buttons.

"Good crazy?" Nico asked.

"Very good crazy." Justine's cheeks still wore a becoming blush. She opened Nico's shirt and her eyes widened slightly. "Very, very good crazy."

Nico kissed her cheek as she pushed the shirt off of him.

"Everyone having fun?" Nora asked. "Say 'no' if you aren't. Say 'hell yes' if you are."

"Oh, hell yes," Justine said.

Nico said, "Hell yes," but he did it in French.

"You're doing that on purpose now," Justine said to him. Nico nodded. "Good. It's working for me."

Nora tapped her tennis shoe with the tip of her riding crop. "Darlings," she said, "less talking, more kissing."

"You heard the woman," Justine said.

Nico apparently had. He took Justine's pretty face in his hands and kissed her long and deep. Nora grinned. They were obedient as two marionettes, and she pulled all their strings. And the best part was, they loved having their strings pulled.

"Neck," Nora said. "You, I mean, Justine. You kiss Nico's neck. He likes that."

He did like that. When Justine put her mouth on his neck over his naked collarbone, Nora saw Nico's eyelashes flutter and his chest heave with a hard breath. Beautiful. Just beautiful.

"Chest," Nora said. Justine kissed his chest. "Arms." Justine kissed his biceps. "Throat," Nora said. Justine kissed his throat.

"Hmm..." Nora said. "What to kiss next?"

"I have a suggestion," Justine said. It seemed her nervousness had evaporated. Nico's too. Both of them simply looked happy and aroused and ready to play.

"I think you're thinking the same thing I'm thinking," Nora said.

"Does it rhyme with 'Rick'?" Justine asked.

"No, it rhymes with 'sock.' But close enough," Nora said. "Nico, love, I want you to come over here." Nora tapped the side of the bed with her riding crop.

Nico obeyed and sat where she'd tapped.

"And you, beautiful," she said to Justine. "I think you should kneel on this." She tapped the ottoman. "And I think I should get in a better position to supervise."

"And lead the cheers?" Justine said.

"Exactly," Nora said. Justine slid the ottoman over to the bed, placing it between Nico's ankles. Nora tapped the ottoman again. She didn't have to say anything. Justine knew what to do. Like a dainty maiden, she lifted the skirt of her red dress and knelt primly on the ottoman.

"I have no other orders for the time being," Nora said. "Other than, have fun, kids."

"Want to have fun?" Justine asked Nico.

"I already am," he said.

Justine bent her head and kissed Nico's side, his ribcage and stomach. Nora tapped the bed with her hand and Nico rolled back.

"I cannot believe I'm doing this," Justine said with an ear-to-ear grin. "I swear I'm usually boring." She unbuttoned Nico's trousers. "I need to hang out in cemeteries more often." Justine glanced down at Nico's gorgeous erection. "Way more often."

Nico inhaled sharply as her blood-red lips surrounded and sucked him. Nora slid onto the bed and sat at his side. She took his hand in hers and kissed his palm as Justine licked his cock from base to tip. Nico's dark eyes were half-closed in pleasure and arousal, but he kept his gaze locked on Nora's.

"I love you, Moosh," she whispered.

He blew her a kiss in reply. No words necessary.

Justine seemed to be having the time of her life with Nico's cock. She lavished it with all the attention it deserved. Nora gave Justine little hints about what to do, how to make Nico feel the best. *Use your hand like this. Use your tongue like that. Stroke harder, softer, longer...* Soon Nico was panting hard. His hips lifted off the bed in small hungry undulations. Justine's red fingernails lightly scoured his stomach, leaving behind pink tracks on his brown skin. Her red tongue massaged every inch of Nico. Nora smiled at the smear of red lipstick on Nico's stomach. It was sexy enough that Nora would have to take a picture of it just to look at longingly when they were apart again.

Nora ran her fingers through his hair, kissed his mouth, his shoulder, his forehead. He was so young and lovely and hers, all hers. Even with his cock in another woman's mouth he was all hers because he was doing this to please her. And it did please her. His trust. His pleasure. His playfulness. She felt so close to him in that moment right before he came when he looked at her with love and adoration and wonder. Then his back arched off the bed, and emptied himself inside Justine with a low grunt.

Though Nora told her she didn't have to swallow, Justine did so eagerly. Nora slipped off the bed and handed Justine a cup of water, which she drank quickly before passing it back to Nora.

"Was that fun, sweetheart?" Nora asked, running her hand over Justine's cider-colored hair. Justine leaned against Nora's stomach. Nora held her close and kissed the top of her head.

"Please move here," Justine said, hugging Nora to her tightly.

"Nico?" Nora asked, still stroking Justine's hair. "What do you think? Want to quit the whole France thing and move to the States?"

Tiredly, happily, Nico began to whistle a few bars of "The Star-Spangled Banner."

CHAPTER THIRTEEN

Nora rewarded Justine for a job well done by pulling out her magic wand—not the sort of wand for doing tricks, unless one counted giving Justine two orgasms a trick. Nora personally classified those as treats.

By the time they'd emptied their glasses, it was two in the morning. They invited Justine to stay the night, but she said she had to get home. There was no way she could tell Grandma, "Sorry, can't come get you your breakfast. I was out all night having a three-some with a French vintner and a dominatrix."

So Nora hugged her and gave her a long kiss goodnight and goodbye. Nico, gallant that he was, walked Justine out to her car.

Nora was half asleep already by the time Nico returned to their room. She heard him undressing but was too tired to open her eyes to watch. Nico crawled into bed with her, lifted her cheerleader skirt and slid his hand into her little black cheerleader panties.

"Can't you see I'm sleeping?" Nora said.

"Keep sleeping," he said. "I don't mind."

"You're wicked," she said as he teased her clitoris with his fingertips.

"Not wicked. Mischievous," he said. It was a gorgeous word to hear in a French accent, especially when whispered into her ear and followed by a kiss on her earlobe.

Nora was too tired to argue with him and, honestly, she didn't care either way. As long as he kept doing that to her with his fingers.

"I need to make love," Nico said.

Nora nodded. Sleepy or not, she wasn't about to tell him no when he needed it. He slid her panties down her legs. If she'd been more awake she would have told him to let her get under the covers so they could avoid staining the Amish quilt again. Ah, too late. He slid one finger along her slit, and Nora forgot all about the Amish.

"You're wet," he said as he nipped at her neck.

"I watched a beautiful woman suck your cock. I told you I liked that sort of thing. Did you?"

"I did," he said, touching her inside with long strokes of his fingers. He massaged her g-spot and Nora started panting. "But only this one time, I think."

"Only once?"

"You're enough for me," he said softly. "Even if you don't think you are, you are. More than enough sometimes."

"Am I a handful?" she asked. He cupped her between the thighs and laughed.

"And a mouthful."

He kissed a path down her body and nestled between her thighs. He started to lick her and Nora raised her head, suddenly wide awake.

"You took out the fangs, right?" she asked.

"Of course," he said.

"Whew. Good, carry on." *Interview* with a vampire was fine. *Intercourse* with a vampire was harrowing.

Nico, defanged, opened her wide with his fingers and began licking her.

"Candy is dandy," Nora said with a sigh of pleasure. "But to lick her is quicker."

As he continued licking her, he murmured

erotic compliments in both English and French. He loved the way she tasted. He loved the way she moved. He loved her pussy, her wetness, the way her clitoris throbbed against his tongue… She came hard, clenching all around his three fingers buried inside of her. It was an intense orgasm and all Nora wanted to do after was sleep. Nico had other ideas.

He moved on top of her. Nora opened her legs even wider for him, and he entered her with a stroke. Her tired eyes fluttered open and she looked up at him braced over her and met his eyes. They didn't say anything. They rarely did on their last night together before they had to part. She liked the silence. She could hear his breathing and her own, hear him moving in her, her own wetness around him, the slight creaking of the bed and the tree branches tapping at the window in the cold autumn wind.

Beautiful boy. Beautiful lovely boy. When they met she'd thought the universe was playing a trick on her and instead it had only a treat for her up its sleeves.

Nico came inside her, releasing a long low groan as he filled her. Afterward, Nora couldn't keep her eyes open another second. She let Nico undress her and put her under the covers. She was seconds from sleep when he came back to bed after his shower and pressed his warm naked body against hers.

"Did we forget anything?" Nora asked as Nico kissed her goodnight.

"We never saw a ghost," he said.

"Ah," she said. "Next year."

And then she was asleep. She dreamed of pretty dancing witches with hair the color of apple cider and woke up smiling.

The smile didn't last long when she saw Nico. He was dressed and standing by the window with his phone in his hand. His posture was tense, his face a closed book.

Nora immediately sat up and pulled the covers to her chest. "What's wrong?"

"I tried to text Justine to make sure she got home safe last night. And, you know, to see she was okay. I got this back."

He held out his phone to Nora. She was worried she'd see a message from Justine asking they never contact her again, or saying something about how she wished she'd never met them. She didn't expect an error message that read the number was no longer in service.

"That can't be right," Nora said, staring at the generic error text he'd received. "We were texting her all day yesterday."

"You try," Nico said.

Nora tried. She got the same message back instantly.

She and Nico met eyes. "This is weird," Nora said. "What's the name of that place she works?"

"Two Keys," Nico said.

"That's it. Let's run over there and ask them if she's okay."

Nora dressed in a hurry and they headed out on foot. It was ten in the morning. They had about an hour before they had to leave town.

"Maybe her phone was stolen," Nora said. "Or maybe it got hacked?"

"Maybe," Nico said.

Two Keys was around the corner from the cemetery. The tavern was open for the brunch crowd, and a line stretched out the door. Nico told her to wait out front while he checked inside.

Nico came out a minute later, a confused and worried look on his face. He shook his head, but didn't meet her eyes. "Something's wrong," he said. "They said…they said they never heard of her."

"How is that possible? She said she was walking home from work. This is the place. The cemetery is right down the block."

"The hostess hadn't heard of her," Nico said. "The bartender says he's worked here five years. Doesn't know any girl with that name."

"Did you describe her?"

He nodded.

Nora had a sinking feeling Justine was giving them the ice-cold shoulder, and had tasked her co-workers with shooing them away. She took a long breath through her nose. Steam rose everywhere. It was cold, bitterly so, and they needed to get Nico to the airport.

"It happens sometimes," Nora said as they turned back toward the B&B. "People think they're ready to be kinky, and they go out and have a wild night. The next morning they wake up wallowing in regret."

"I walked her out to her car," Nico said, bewildered. "She had fun."

"You just never know," Nora said. She could have sworn Justine was cool. She seemed so cool and nice and sexy and fun and funny. She seemed like a perfect date.

Nico stopped at the cemetery's iron gates, shrugged, and walked through.

"What are you doing?" she asked. "The girl ditched us. She—"

"I'm taking the shortcut," he said. "And we saw her here first. You never know…"

A thousand questions ran through her head as they entered St. Patrick's and started down the main path. The worst part was that this was all Nora's fault. She'd dragged Nico into it. Nico was so quiet now that it made Nora nervous. She hated when he shut down like that. Was he blaming himself? Did he think they'd pushed their new friend too far? Did he blame Nora?

They made it all the way through the small cemetery without seeing another soul. They walked out the gate and Nico came to a dead stop in the middle of the sidewalk.

"What's—" Nora stopped when she saw what he saw. It was a missing-persons poster, torn and faded and water-stained, stapled to a telephone pole. In thick marker at the top it read:

Have you seen this woman? Last seen October 22, 2004. Reward. Please bring our daughter home.

The grainy black and white photograph was unmistakably Justine. Same eyes. Same hair style. Same wide, bright smile. Either she hadn't aged in the past decade, or…

"That's not possible," Nora said, her blood turning to ice.

Nico had his hand over his mouth. His eyes were wide. He seemed incapable of speech.

"No way," Nora said. "Not a chance. I kissed her. You kissed her. We all fooled around. We spent hours together. She drank your wine. I gave her one of my books. She...she had a grandmother. She..."

"We met her in the cemetery," Nico said. "We didn't hear her behind us. It was like she came out of nowhere."

"This is not possible. This is not... Oh my God."

There was no way in hell Justine was a ghost. No way. None.

But if Nora actually believed it wasn't possible at all in the least, why was she shaking?

The Smiling Girl... People say she'll walk next to them if they're foolish enough to take a stroll through the graveyard at midnight...

"I can't..." Nora put her hand to her forehead.

Suddenly, Nora's phone buzzed with a new message. She nearly dropped it in her rush to read it.

The message was from Justine's number.

But it wasn't a message so much as a series of screenshots of a text conversation between Justine and Nico—a text conversation wherein they planned an elaborate set-up late last night to scare the shit out of Nora.

Nora stared at the message, and then looked up at Nico, whose eyes were now glowing with near-satanic joy.

"You…little…shit," she said.

He burst into laughter.

"You son of a bitch. You…"

"I asked 'trick or treat' last night and you said 'trick,'" Nico reminded her. "It's your own fault."

Nora raised her fists at him. He was still laughing.

Monster. Asshole. Bastard. Motherfucker. She called him every last name in the book, and then a few more. She was going to take him back to their suite and flog him seven ways to Sunday and she didn't care if he missed his flight. He could swim back to France for all she cared.

Nora reached out and grabbed him by the lapels of his jacket. "And you know what else?"

"What?" he asked. He was almost crying from the force of his laughter.

She kissed him. She kissed the breath out

of him. Then she let him go so fast he had to grab the cemetery wall behind him to steady himself. She took his face in his hands and pinched his cheeks.

"I am so damn proud of you."

FIN.

COMING AND GOING

ora didn't want to leave. But who would?

She gazed out the window next to the bed and stared at the snowy French countryside. The winery's vines were so white they looked frosted in cake icing. The hills that surrounded the house were like the backs of sleeping white elephants. The frost on the windowpane had been hand-painted there by Jack Frost and Robert Frost had written a poem about it.

Such incredible beauty…it was a gift. She lived in New Orleans, where it never, ever snowed (except when it did). Nora felt as spoiled as a king's youngest daughter. She didn't deserve such beauty—who did? But she did appreciate it. She might be spoiled but she was no brat.

There was a brat in the house who was a brat for no other reason than he was twenty-six and she was thirty-seven. How dare her lover be eleven years younger than she was? Rude, unkind, uncalled for…she ought to wake him just to spank him. Except she wouldn't, since he looked so lovely while he was sleeping.

Besides, he hated being spanked. The whip or the cane or ten different floggers in a row—anything but spanking, he said. So she never spanked him.

Well, not very often. Spoiled rotten brat.

The brat in question was named Nico, and she wanted to wake him and order him to make love to her, but it was only four in the morning. Oh, she'd wake him for that, but she'd let him sleep a little longer. She left for the airport in only two hours and she couldn't sleep thinking about the coming long separation from him. The day was January thirtieth. She wouldn't see him again until April. She'd leave him in winter and the next time they kissed it would be spring.

She kissed his cheek gently enough not to wake him and slipped out of bed. Nico lived in an old stone country house in the south of France. What it lacked in modern conveniences it made up for in beauty and charm—almost. But tell that to her ice-cube toes as she crept downstairs in her nightgown to make tea. She should have packed her wool socks and knitted shawls. Who knew it snowed in wine country?

She heated up the tea kettle and when ready, poured the boiling water into a large earthenware mug. Nora didn't really want the tea—chamomile. She wanted the heat. Carefully, she cradled the mug in her hands as she climbed up the steep wooden stairs to their bedroom.

Our bedroom. Nico had called it that last night. *Do you want me to do anything to our bedroom before you come back?* He'd been asking if she wanted him to paint or move the furniture, make room for her things in his closet. But she couldn't answer. The "our" had meant so much to her, it had taken her words away from her. She'd merely shaken her head "no." Later, she told him their bedroom—with its big oak bed and ancient quilts—was *parfait.*

She'd shared her bed before. Many, many times. But she'd never shared a bedroom. Never married. Never lived with a lover. Separate worlds. Separate lives. *His* bedroom. *Her* bedroom. Only with Nico had a room in a house ever been "ours."

And so it was with a smile on her face she stepped into their bedroom, holding the mug of hot tea in her hands. When her palms were sufficiently heated, she set the mug aside and knelt on the floor by the bed like a child saying her bedtime prayers. She put her hot hands on Nico's ice-cold face—one on his forehead, the other on his cheek—and let the soft heat and the tender touch wake him gently.

As she waited for his eyes to open, she

studied him in the winter moonlight. His skin was brown, his hair black. His eyes were what she called "celadon," though she wasn't sure a word existed to perfectly describe that green glassy color. When Nico woke at last, he scolded her the way a serious child scolds a frivolous adult.

"What are doing up?" he demanded. "You'll freeze. Get back in bed."

"Yes, sir," she said. A tease. She owned him and not the other way around.

He held up the blankets—a flannel sheet, a fleece comforter, a double wedding ring quilt as old as the house—and she slid in next to his naked body. He'd lived in the south of France his entire life. He was acclimated to the cold. He pulled her close and murmured into her ear, "What time is it?"

"I leave in two hours," she said. All their time was measured backward from the moment she had to leave to the present moment.

"What do we do until then?" he asked, though he already knew the answer.

"I want you inside me," she said. He, of course, moved to obey at once. One of the perks of dating a twenty-six-year-old.

He lifted her nightgown to her hips. He loved her nightgowns, the more prim and prissy the better. He loved having something to push up, to lift, to slide a hand under, to unbutton, to untie, to open, to grip with rough fingers, to pull off over her head and toss across the room. He didn't just love to see her, he'd said of her schoolmarm nighttime attire. He loved *unveiling* her. He loved to work for her. He loved the tease.

He parted her legs with his hand and cupped her vulva, pressing his palm into her clitoris as his mouth found her mouth.

Her brat knew how to kiss. All his lovers had been older women—a fetish, but a good one in her opinion. They'd taught him well. He kissed like fire and she pushed her hips into his hand was he pressed his tongue past her lips. She forgot all about the frost on the window and the icy wood floors and the snow on the vines. Outside, it was January. In the bed, it was summer. The blankets were a tropical island. The sheets lay atop the surface of the sun.

Nico slid on top of her and pushed his cock against the entrance of her vagina. She lifted her hips, tilting them at the precise angle necessary to take every inch of him all the way into her. He wrapped his arms around her lower back and held her in place, in that precise place and entered her straight and true.

"Ahh…" he breathed, the exact sound she made when she'd wrapped her cold hands around the mug.

"Don't come," she said, hotly breathing the order into his ear. He laughed softly. "Don't come. Don't come. Don't come."

He grinned down at her, a grin that said *silly woman.* "I can last longer than ten seconds inside of you."

"I mean, don't come at all. Not until I tell you."

"When?" he asked.

"*If,*" she said. "Not *when.*"

His grin was gone. Hers remained in place.

Theirs was a new love, less than a year old, and that baby love was still learning how to walk and say its first words. She was Nico's first dominant, his first sadist. Learning how to submit to a woman had been a challenge. But he had the one trait all teachers seek in a prize pupil—he loved to learn.

"If," he said, nodding.

"Get on with it," she said, waving her hand. "Fuck me. I didn't put your cock in me for my health."

He laughed again and started to move in her. For a few minutes they did nothing but breathe and fuck. Nico could fuck as well as he could kiss. He thrust deep and slow into her, dragging it out and always at the necessary angle so that the shaft of his cock grazed her clitoris going in, grazed it again coming out. He knew how to fuck her long and hard without their bodies ever separating. When he went in, he stayed in.

Nora closed her eyes and clung to his upper arms as she worked herself up and down on his cock. Her heels dug deep into the soft mattress as she pushed up, up, up, and against him. Up, up, up, helping him to fuck her deeper, rougher. Up, up, up, she heard his cock moving inside her wetness.

"Shit," he said, but in French. *Merde*. He dropped his head onto her shoulder. "I have to stop for a second."

"You can," she said. "But stay inside me."

He stayed in her pussy, but rolled the both of them onto their sides to ease the pressure. He was panting. She stroked his chest with her fingernails. *Poor boy*, she thought but did not say. *Poor mistreated boy.*

"You're so wet," he said, his hand in her hair. "It's killing me. I want to die in you."

Ah, the French. *La petite morte*. The little death. The orgasm.

"And I want you to live in me. And I own you, so I win."

"Don't you want my come?" he asked, pouting.

"I always want your come," she said. "I want it on my breasts, and I want you to rub it into my skin. I want it on my stomach and on my back. And sometimes I want it in my mouth so I can swallow it. And I want it deep in my pussy. Sometimes in my ass. I always want it. Every drop of it in—"

He groaned and buried his head against her chest. His little gambit had backfired on him. She chuckled like a super-villain in a cartoon.

"You must hate me," he said.

"Did you know a man's sperm can live inside a uterus for a couple of days?" she asked. "Sometimes when you're out of the house working and I'm alone in here, maybe reading by the fireplace, I think about how your sperm is still inside me hours and hours after we last had sex. And it makes me very happy to know it's inside me."

He groaned again until he laughed. "Did you insult a witch? Is that what happened to you? You insulted a witch and she stole your heart?"

"Two days from now, I'll be all the way across the Atlantic Ocean, lying in my bed in my house in New Orleans, and your sperm will still be inside me."

"If you let me come," he said.

"Right," she said. "If."

"And if I come before you tell me I can?"

"You wouldn't," she said, stroking his sweat-dampened hair.

"No, I wouldn't." He met her eyes and she saw the determination in them, the determination to please her or die trying. Ah, her boy was learning.

"Good boy," she said.

He raised his fingers to the buttons at her throat.

"Are you sure that's a good idea?" she asked as he slowly opened the buttons of her prim nightgown.

"If I'm going to be tortured," he said, "I want to be tortured with your nipples in my mouth."

Fair point. She allowed him to pull the gown off her shoulders, to bare her breasts to him. He took her left breast in hand, cupped it and lifted it. Nora sighed with pleasure as he suckled her. She ran her fingers through his thick wavy hair and pressed her hips into his. On their sides, facing each other, they slowly fucked as Nico kissed her breasts.

"You know why I torture you like this?" she asked.

He shook his head, but didn't answer. His mouth was full of her.

"Because I'm in love with you," she said. He smiled and kept right on suckling. "There's a saying—you always hurt the one you love. It's especially true for sadists. I never grew past the stage where girls kick the boys they have crushes on."

"You have a crush on me?" he asked, pausing between swirling licks of his tongue around her nipple.

"Your cock's inside me. Is that really a surprise?"

"It never hurts to hear," he said and returned to her nipples.

"Yes, I have a crush on you, you twerp."

"What's a twerp?" he asked. They were always stumbling across English words he didn't know.

"You," she said. "You're a twerp."

"So a twerp is a handsome young man who is good in bed?"

"Precisely," she said. He grinned before attaching her breasts again with renewed intensity.

Nora was not about to lay down for that.

She rolled Nico onto his back and straddled him, hands on his chest to steady herself.

Nico groaned loudly as she moved her hips on his cock.

"Good?" she asked.

"You're evil," he said.

"You're just figuring that out?"

She pulled off the gown and balled it up, tossing it over her head like a basketball player performing a trick shot.

"I'm going to ride your cock for..." She pretended to check her watch. "...a long time."

"Can I come?"

"Don't come. Don't come. Oh, and don't come."

Nico nodded, took a shallow breath. He looked like a man being led toward a firing squad. Nora would have felt sorry for him if she hadn't been so turned on.

She rocked her hips on him and his cock shifted inside her as she moved. Nico's hands lay on her upper thighs, but as she pushed against him, his fingers tightened their grip on her. Poor boy. Poor sweet boy.

Nora stroked his chest while she fucked him from on top, rubbed his chest and scored it with her fingernails. He wasn't much of a masochist—not yet, anyway—but he did love being scratched. Red fingernail marks—claw marks—made him feel wanted, he'd said. If she left red marks on his stomach, he'd lift his shirt every time he went to the bathroom to see the marks in the mirror. It made him feel like he was so desirable to her that she lost control of herself during sex and turned into an animal.

She rode his cock hard as his grip on her hips tightened. Nora gazed at him as she rode him, at his fingers digging deep into her thighs, at his head on the pillow, at his closed eyes, at those perfect sculpted lips of his slightly parted as he panted, panted like a man in pain. Ah, she'd think of this sight on the plane.

"Why are your eyes closed?" she asked.

"I'm thinking of the last time I had the stomach flu," he said. "It's helping."

"Was it bad?"

"It wasn't as much fun as you riding my cock."

"Well," she said, "what is?"

He opened his eyes and laced his fingers behind the back of his head. "Nothing," he said, but in French. *Rien.*

Nora leaned in and kissed his lovely mouth that said such lovely words in such a lovely language. He wrapped her in his arms and held her close.

Slowly, she rolled her hips in a tight spiral, clenching her inner muscles around his cock. "Don't come," she said. "Don't come. Don't come. Don't come."

"Don't go," he said. "Don't go. Don't go. Don't go."

Nora stopped moving. She pulled back and down at him, tears in her eyes. "I have to go," she said.

"I know," he said. He gathered her long black hair in his hands and pulled it off her face, held it at the nape of her neck so he could kiss her throat. "But I had to try."

"You know I can't go unless you let me," she said.

"You think I wouldn't drive you to the airport?"

"You know what I mean."

"So..." He wagged his finger at her. "You're in charge of my coming," he said. "And I'm charge of your going?"

"Only fair, right?"

"I might not let you go," he said.

"Well, I might not let you come, either." With that, Nora slipped off of him, separating their bodies.

"What?" he asked. "What's wrong?"

"Nothing. Let's take a long hot bath together before we have to leave for the airport."

She ran their bath and they held each other in the steaming water, kissing and touching and scrubbing and laughing. After breakfast, they piled her luggage into his Land Rover and headed to the airport.

He drove. She sat in the passenger seat. He kept his hands on the wheel. She kept her hand on his knee. They didn't speak for the first fifteen minutes.

"I didn't mean to kill your boner," he said.

"I have got to stop teaching you English phrases and not telling you what they mean," she said, shaking her head.

"I know what it means. I meant, you know, what's it called—lady boner?"

"I never dreamed 'lady boner' would sound so good in a French accent."

"Nora," he said, turning his head quickly to look at her before putting his eyes back on the road where they belonged.

"I love you," she said. "I shouldn't, but I do. You're eleven years younger than I am, and you live across the fucking ocean."

"What were you thinking?" he asked, shaking his head.

"I wanted to play with you this morning because it was either laugh or cry. And then you had to go and be wonderful and sweet." She sighed heavily. "Never do it again."

She squeezed his knee. He lifted her hand off his leg and raised it to his lips. One kiss. Enough said. They drove the rest of the way to the airport in tender silence, Nora's hand on Nico's knee, Nico's hand on her hand.

One hand on the wheel.

They arrived at the airport and Nico started to park in the closest spot.

"Not here," Nora said. She scanned the parking lot, saw a large paneled van. "Next to that one."

He raised his eyebrow but did as he was told. The boy was learning.

He parked, turned off the engine.

"Leave it on," Nora said.

Then he knew what was happening. Nora glanced out the window. No one around.

"Backseat?" he asked.

"Backseat," she said.

In seconds, they were on the bench seat and tearing into each other. Nora yanked Nico's thick leather jacket off and tossed it into the front seat. He reached under her tight black turtleneck sweater and unhooked her bra. He yanked her skirt up. She hadn't bothered with panties, only stockings and garters since she knew this would happen. Of course it would happen. If she wanted something to happen, it happened.

Lying on her back in the cramped back-seat, she reached for his belt, his jeans button. He was so hard his cock popped out when she unzipped him, already hard as a rock and straining toward her. He yanked her skirt up and pushed her thighs wide. She raised her hips in invitation. He spread her vulva open at the seam and positioned his cock at the hole. With a rough thrust he was in her and after that there was no talking, no kissing, no sweetness, no love.

Only fucking.

He pushed her sweater and bra up to her neck as he rode her hard into the worn leather seat. The cock in her was brutal. He was pistoning into her, vicious as a jackhammer. She was barely aware of him kissing her nipples or pinching them or sucking them. There was only the thick organ pounding into her, almost angrily, and the little explosions in her throbbing clitoris, the contractions of her vagina as he speared her.

She slid her hands into his jeans, cupped his perfect twenty-six-year-old ass in her two hands and felt as his muscles tightened to iron bands as he rutted on her. He drove his cock into her pussy like a nail into soft wood.

She dug her hands into his flesh as he pounded her, goading him on with quiet commands. *Harder, harder...*

It didn't seem possible he could fuck her any harder, but they found a way.

He grabbed her leg, pushed it so wide she had to wrap her knee around the front seat. She was so open he could have fisted her to the wrist if she'd wanted him to. And she did want him to, so she told him to...

Nico's chest heaved at the order. He didn't answer, just dug his teeth into the strap of his watch band on his right wrist and wrenched it off. She would remember the image of his teeth at his wrist, his teeth biting leather on her death bed.

He brought his fingers together and pushed the tips into her vagina. The hole widened as he pressed in, and her inner muscles spread as he pushed. Nora grabbed the headrest of the driver's seat and the door handle behind her to steady herself as he twisted and turned his fingers until he'd pushed past the knuckles, the palm, finally the wrist. When it was all in, she looked down and saw his hand splitting her wide open. She felt so filled she would burst. He fucked her with his hand, lifting her hips from the inside. Every knuckle of his hand brushed every nerve in her cunt. She came hard with a quick vicious spasm that brought her shoulders off the seat.

She panted, gulping huge breaths as he worked his hand carefully out of her.

"Can I come?" he asked. Asked and begged, begged and pleaded.

"Yes, you can come," she said.

He turned her onto her hands and knees. He wrapped his arm around her waist and entered her from behind. For about ten seconds, there was nothing happening in the whole wide world except his cock slamming into her and his testicles brushing against her still-throbbing clit with each thrust.

He held her breasts, squeezing them roughly as he slammed into her hard enough to shake the car down to the chassis. He grunted his breaths, whimpered once, and then went silent. When he came, she knew it was happening because he said her name, but he wasn't saying it to her. He was simply saying it.

Nora...

When he pulled out of her, she winced. Thick warm semen that poured from her. Nico staunched the flow with a handkerchief out of his jeans pocket. She took it from him and pressed it between her thighs as she straightened her clothes, hooked her bra, ran her fingers through her hair.

Nico sat back and watched her, silent. She turned and kissed him, but only quickly. If it were a long kiss, she'd never leave.

"Can I go?" she asked.

He grazed her cheek with the back of his knuckles.

"Yes," he said. "You can go."

Tiffany Reisz is the *USA Today* bestselling author of the Romance Writers of America RITA®-winning Original Sinners series.

Her erotic fantasy *The Red*—the first entry in the Godwicks series, self-published under the banner 8th Circle Press—was named an NPR Best Book of the Year and a Goodreads Best Romance of the Month.

Tiffany lives in Kentucky with her husband, author Andrew Shaffer, and two cats. The cats are not writers.

Subscribe to the Tiffany Reisz email newsletter to stay up-to-date with new releases, ebook discounts, and signed books:

www.tiffanyreisz.com/mailing-list

www.ingramcontent.com/pod-product-compliance
Lightning Source LLC
Chambersburg PA
CBHW030756200726
48288CB00004B/1210